The Jill Crewe Miscellany No. One

by Jemma Spark

Epona Publishing

www.ponybookuniverse.com
www.books.by/jemmaspark

Table of Contents

Synopses of the Jill Books

Book 1 – *Jill Rides Cross-Country*

Jill Crewe has lived in a perfect world of ponies and gymkhanas in a small English village, Chatton. Discouraged from a career with horses, she is about to reluctantly go off to secretarial college when her life is turned upside down. Her mother announces that she is getting married again and they are going to live in a Scottish Highland castle, with hundreds of acres of moorland, stables, an indoor riding school and a cross-country course. Jill feels that she has to prove her worth as a person, not only to herself, but also to her new-found relations, as she prepares to enter adult equestrian competitions.

Book 2 – *Jill Has Two Horses*

Jill Crewe has left Chatton and is now living in a Scottish Highland castle with her mother and new stepfather. She has a beautiful young grey horse, Balius, but she yearns for an older, trained mount so she can compete in open events in the coming year. She accepts a job as a secretary to Bryony Peach in Cornwall in order to earn money towards the purchase of a second horse. She drives from Scotland to Cornwall to begin work, taking Balius with her and stopping along the way with various horsey characters such as Ned Sperrit - a horse dealer, Charles a racehorse trainer and his glamorous wife, Venetia, and the Merrivales – a jolly family of five children living on Dartmoor. In Cornwall she finds herself drawn into the smuggling activities of an unlikely bunch of criminals.

Book 3 – *Jill Goes Pony Trekking*

Jill is planning to go pony trekking with the Merrivales, reliving some of the idyllic moments of her youth. But she has this happy knack of falling into adventure and along the way she gets mixed up with an extremely handsome but mysterious young man. Then there are people after them and they need to disguise themselves before they dash to Dartmoor.

Book 4 – *Jill and the Steeplechaser*

Jill Crewe is a young woman living in rural England during the early 1960s. In previous books her charmed childhood in Chatton with her two ponies Black Boy and Rapide, was described. In her spare time she wrote pony books about her real life. Teetering on the edge of adulthood she moved to the Scottish Highlands to live in a castle when her mother married Richard Micheldever. Moving on from ponies to horses she is now the owner of Balius, a magnificent thoroughbred cross Highland gelding, and a sweet chestnut mare, Copperplate. This is the fourth book in Jemma Spark's Jill series and our heroine goes back to Chatton to live in her original home, Pool Cottage. Her best friend Ann Derry is emotionally wrecked from a love affair gone wrong and goes to stay with her. Their life of horsey adventures, and sometimes misadventures continue. Jill acquires a steeplechaser and enters a point-to-point to try race riding. In order to qualify to enter the race Jill has to foxhunt and after her first enthusiasm she is forced to grapple with a moral dilemma when faced with anti-blood sport protests. A host of original characters parade through the pages including the Cholly-Sawcutt sisters, Jill's old enemy Susan Pyke, Wendy Mead the instructor at Mrs Darcy's riding school, James and Diana Bush, Jill's cousin Cecilia and many more.

Book 5 – *Jill Dreams of a Dressage Horse*

Jill Crewe returns to England after a month of dressage training in Germany and is beset with a burning ambition to buy her own dressage horse and compete at the highest levels. During her childhood she dreamed of jumping in the open jumping at Chatton Show, now she wants to represent England in the dressage competitions at the Olympics. She is scheduled to work as an assistant to the Master of the Horse while the film *Macbeth* is being shot at her home Blainstock Castle, in the Scottish Highlands. By chance, she finds a dressage horse right under her nose and can think of nothing but how to raise the huge amount of money that she needs to buy it.

Book 6 – *Jill and the Horsemasters*

Jill Crewe has just acquired a fantastic dressage horse, and she is determined that she will compete at the highest levels. It is the early 1960s, and her ambition is to Ride for England. She also wants to become an equestrian journalist and is offered the chance to write dressage articles for Horse and Hound. Until now, Jill has avoided the irksome issue of romance, but at this stage of her life she finds herself in the grip of an infatuation for a dashing and accomplished horseman. Training her dressage horse, pursuing a career as a journalist, and attracting a handsome man lead her into a series of madcap adventures and misadventures.

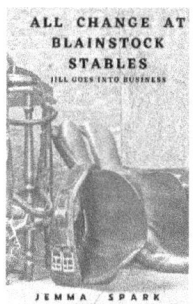

Book 7 – *All Change at Blainstock Stables: Jill Goes Into Business*

Jill Crewe returns to Blainstock Stables after completing the Horsemasters Course at Porlock Vale. She takes her German friend, Dieter with her to spend Christmas at the castle. Stopping off in London to show Dieter the sights, she visits her literary agent to receive some unsettling news. Expecting a happy festive Christmas, she has to come to terms with drastic changes, which are affecting the lives of everyone at the castle. There is to be a new social order, and huge challenges to face.

Jill's Ponies: Black Boy and Rapide
By Jemma Spark

Book 8 – *Jill's Ponies: Black Boy and Rapide*

Jill Crewe lived in a small village, Chatton, during the 1950s and enjoyed an idyllic life riding ponies, having adventures and attending gymkhanas. She grows up and has to sell her two beloved ponies, Black Boy and Rapide. They went to the same family so that they could be together but then had to be sold on separately. This story picks up on the ponies' lives with their new owners. Lavender Ellison-Heath is a young girl, a single child with a mother who wants her to win in gymkhanas so that she can gain entry to the local county set. She has learned to ride on Black Boy and has had some riding lessons from Jill Crewe. Rapide now belongs to Morgan Pevensy, the youngest child of the horse-mad Pevensy family. She has inherited Rapide from her sister Porsche who is going to compete in adult riding classes. This book follows on from Ruby Ferguson and Jemma Spark's Jill books which have followed the life of Jill Crewe. Now the focus is on the ponies and what happens to them.

The Adventures
of Jill's Ponies

by Jemma Spark

Book 9 – *The Adventures of Jill's Ponies*

This is not only the story of the adventures of Black Boy and Rapide, Jill Crewe's ponies, but many of the horse people who live in Chatton, a village in Oxfordshire in the early 1960s. It is the sequel to *Jill's Ponies:*

Black Boy and Rapide. There is a pony club rally, a point-to-point at Grassmere, a Christmas party at Pevensy Park and Tiddington Hunter Trials.

Susan King (née Pyke) is unhappily married to a small town solicitor, a dull stick, and has become infatuated with Austin Pevensy, the dashing but careless second son of the Duke and Duchess of Tolkington. Mark Lansdowne, who is related to Jill through her mother's second marriage, has become enamoured of Mercedes Pevensy. The loveable, eccentric, old women, Felicia and Jessica Farthington run an animal refuge and have a promising eventer living in their dining room. Mrs Darcy is back and expanding the business of her riding school. Jill is en route to Australia and spends a week in Chatton before she leaves. She arrives to find that Black Boy has been stolen and she is determined to find him.

Book 10 - *Jill and the Prize Winners*

The magazine, *Riding*, has run a competition and six winners have been selected to go to Blainstock Castle for two weeks to compete for the grand prize, a weekend for two at the Spanish Riding School in Vienna. The winners include Charles Ravenscroft, Susan Barington-Brown, Lettie Lonsdale, Janet Fawley, Patrick Huntingdon and Rennie Jordan. They take part in a number of competitions and a grand prize winner is selected. While they're still at the castle, a couple from America and their horse trainer arrive, having rented the Dower House for a year. Jill has just returned from Australia, where she was on a showjumping tour. She helps with the organisation of the prize winners' activities but finds herself caught up in the drama of the new arrivals and has to make some drastic decisions.

Who's Who in the Jill books

SPOILER ALERT – INFORMATION CONTAINED IN THIS SECTION WILL REVEAL DEVELOPMENTS IN RELATIONSHIPS AND EVENTS THAT OCCUR THROUGH THE COURSE OF THE FIRST TEN JILL BOOKS. SO, IF YOU ARE READING FROM BOOK 1 AND HAVEN'T YET GOT TO BOOK 10, THEN YOU MAY LEARN OF DEVELOPMENTS THAT OCCUR IN THE LATER BOOKS.

HUMANS

Adrian - a friend of James Bush who went out with Wendy Mead for a short time. He wanted her to be a housewife and she wished to continue with an equestrian career so the relationship did not develop.

Agnes Pevensy – the Duchess of Tolkington, known to all as 'Aggie', she is the mistress of the large estate, Pevensy Park. She has always been horse-mad, has five children, and is a force to be reckoned with, a powerful matriarch.

Alan Twistlethaite – Richard Micheldever's childhood friend who is his best man when he marries Catherine, Jill Crewe's mother.

Amanda Applewood – a young woman who tricked Jill, as a young teenager, to go and stay with the Lockett family and ride her pony, Plum. (original Ruby Ferguson character)

Amelia – a friend of Gwyneth Smith. She is an unprepossessing young woman with short mousy hair and wears mannish clothing. She was a guest at Blainstock Castle when the mare Jewel went missing.

Angela - a young girl who rides her own pony Christie for riding lessons at Mrs Darcy's riding school, a member of the Birtle Pony Club.

Angela Cartwright – a student at Porlock Vale, a mother of three children who is pursing her dream of becoming an equestrian professional.

Ann Derry – famous for being Jill Crewe's best friend, currently studying at college so that she can gain entry to Bristol Veterinary College. Her boyfriend is Henry Thurston, the local vet. She lives at Pool Cottage. (original Ruby Ferguson character)

April Cholly-Sawcutt – once as round as a bouncing ball, she is now slim, the eldest of the three Cholly-Sawcutt sisters, the daughter of Captain Cholly-Sawcutt, engaged to Gary Horton, who is running her father's showjumping yard. (original Ruby Ferguson character)

Ariel Bergman – a student at Porlock Vale, a blonde beauty from Scandinavia.

Arleen – lives in the Scottish Highlands, is an artist and the girlfriend of John who was the groom at Blainstock Castle, before he became a partner in the Blainstock Riding Stables business.

Arthur Branson - , a nondescript guest who stays at Blainsock Casle, dressed in very mundane clothes, he is interested in the history of the castle.

Audrey – young Blainstock Riding Stables student, she is very serious, not a good rider and wears spectacles. She is nine-years old in *All Change at Blainstock Stables.*

Augusta Frobisher – Stable Manager at Porlock Vale Stables. She hates 'Sloth'.

The Honourable Austin Pevensy – the second eldest son, younger brother of Royce and Mercedes, and older brother of Porsche and Morgan. He sporadically attends Lonsdale College at Oxford. He is a reasonably good, but rather reckless, rider who competes in point-to-points and hunter trials. He doesn't take anything seriously, good-humoured and glamorous but careless of the welfare of other people. He has a fling with Susan King (née Pyke). He and his younger sister, Porsche, are often in cahoots.

Barty King – married to Susan Pyke, a solicitor in a Rychester firm. He is a dry stick and his sole ambition is to be a partner in the firm.

Beatrice Garter – a forgetful grey-haired woman with enormous owl-like glasses, who works for *Horse and Hound*. She arranges for Jill to go Porlock Vale to write an article in *Jill and the Horsemasters*.

Beau Carlisle – a handsome young actor, whose real name is Alistair McDonald. When Jill met him, he was pretending to be his cousin, Mungo McDonald. He goes to Dartmoor with Jill when the press is after him. Later, he plays the part of Banquo in the film *Macbeth* which is made at Blainstock Castle.

Belinda Bliss – very glamorous and attractive American woman who looks out for Willow Vetch.

Bert Clasher – a National Hunt trainer, who is a friend of Richard Micheldever.

Bert Munro – stable manager at Pevensy Park stables.

Beryl Tainton – friend of Aggie Pevensy, rides in show hunter classes.

Bevan St John – a promising young jump jockey who has a fall and suffered permanent injury that prevents him from ever riding again. He works for the magazine *Riding* and is sent to Blainstock Castle to report on the competition being run there.

Billie Dudgeon – an unscrupulous relative of Ruby Swope, who kept Black Boy hidden when Ruby stole him, then sold him illegally to the Streets.

Lady Blatch-Kiddington – A hostess of house parties who has regularly invited Jack Laskey to stay.

Bob Nutley – a Porlock Vale student from Tavistock.

Bobby – beginner rider, just off the lead rein, one of the Blainstock Riding Stables students. Ten years old in *All Change at Blainstock Stables*.

Bridie McIver – the eldest of the four McIver children whose parents run the general store in the small village near Blainstock Castle. She has bright red hair and loves ponies. She is twelve-years old in *All Change at Blainstock Stables*.

Bryony Peach – an older woman who lives at Lamorna Cove in Cornwall. She employs Jill as a secretary, to complete her memoirs.

Buster Scobie – a landowner who lives near Pevensy Park, a good friend of Royce Pevensy, married to Gertrude.

Buttons Merrivale – the youngest son in the family of five children who live on a farm at Dartmoor.

Mrs Buzzby – the shop owner of the general store in Chatton.

Colonel Butterworth – Chief Instructor of Birtle Pony Club.

Carmela – the beautiful Argentinian girlfriend of Horatio Lansdowne.

Cassie Frayne – Blainstock Riding Stables' student, blue eyes, curly blonde hair, conceited and irritating. Waiting for her mother to buy her the perfect show pony. She is twelve-years old in *All Change at Blainstock Stables*.

Catherine Micheldever – mother of Jill Crewe, wife of Richard Micheldever, mother of young Hamish. (original Ruby Ferguson character)

Cecilia Talbot – Jill's cousin, her mother, Primrose is Catherine's sister. Jill considers her rather a blot as she likes pressing dead flowers, knitting, embroidery, handing out cups of tea at her mother's tea parties. She becomes engaged to Royce Pevensy, and will be the Duchess of Tolkington when his father dies. (original Ruby Ferguson character)

Charles Delphinton – lives near Cheltenham, a racehorse trainer, married to Venetia. Jill stays with them when she is travelling south to work for Bryony Peach.

Charles Ravenscroft – young man from Oxfordshire who goes to Blainstock Castle as a prize winner in a competition run by the magazine *Riding*. He has a damaged leg due to having suffered from poliomyelitis, but has taken up showjumping and has competed in Foxhunter competitions. When he is at Blainstock he falls in love with Susan Barington-Brown. (original Josephine Pullein Thompson character)

Charlie Moreton – much older husband of Clarissa, owns a jump racing stable near Cambridge.

Chumly – a young man with a round face and pudding bowl haircut who had been Cecilia's partner at social occasions.

Captain Cholly-Sawcutt – once competed on the international showjumping stage representing Britain, now has dementia. (original Ruby Ferguson character)

Claire – long-suffering maid of the Ellison-Heaths, forced to wear a ridiculous black and white uniform.

Clarabell Street – the young girl whose father bought Black Boy, when he was sold by one Ruby Swope's unscrupulous relatives, Billy Dudgeon.

Clarissa Moreton (née Dandleby) – one of Cecilia's friends, she has married one of her father's friends called Charlie Morton, who runs a jump racing stable. (original Ruby Ferguson character)

Lady Cynthia Bentick-Throssel - one of the ladies at the dressage course at Porlock Vale. She is the leader of the pack, brays the loudest and elbow aside her inferiors.

David Staley – a professional showjumper who lives in Yeovil. His training methods are dubious and Jill leaves abruptly, not completely a series of lessons that her stepfather had arranged for her.

Mrs Darcy – ran the local Chatton riding school. When she is away Wendy Mead is in charge. (original Ruby Ferguson character)

David – Jill Crewe and her mother's literary agent in London.

Dean - the boyfriend of Jecca, the great-niece of Bryony Peach. He and Jecca are involved in dog smuggling in Cornwall. Jill is drawn into the activity and gets paid for driving them around delivering the dogs.

Mrs Derry – Ann Derry's mother, a worrier. (original Ruby Ferguson character)

The Honourable Diana Barton-Tompkin – one of Mark Lansdowne's girlfriends. She has icy blue eyes and is very toffy-nosed and looks down on, and mocks, Jill when she first goes to Blainstock Castle.

Diana Bush – a lifelong friend of Ann and Jill, the sister of James, a good rider but not ambitious in the equestrian field. (original Ruby Ferguson character)

Dieter Schunker – a young man who lives in a village near Munich in Germany. Jill Crewe meets him when they are studying a Porlock Vale. She takes him to Blainstock for Christmas.

Lord Dimpleton – the uncle of Gwyneth Smith, aka the Countess of Waverton. Gwynnie's mare Jewel and her colt, Goldie are kept on his estate.

Dinah Dean – a determined young girl who rescued the ponies that were going to slaughter in one of the original Jill books by Ruby Ferguson. She was adopted by Mrs Whirley at Blossom Park and sent to boarding school. She is now studying law at Cambridge University, an anti-blood sports advocate. She goes to Cecilia's engagement party with Simon Caxton-Thorpe. (original Ruby Ferguson character)

Mrs Dinwiddie-Marsh - one of the ladies at the dressage course at Porlock Vale that Jill attends.

Dorrie Cannon – one of the Australian twins who has 'riding lessons' from Jill Crewe when they are visiting one of their relatives in England. (original Ruby Ferguson character)

Dougie – a young boy of unprepossessing appearance with a huge nose, wide-blown nostrils and pancake freckles. Owns a grey pony of Welsh and Arab breeding and has lessons at Mrs Darcy's riding school.

Edwina – a girl Jill went to school with. She fell in love with a boy called Rupert and gave up ponies.

Elisabeth Thornton – sister of Henry Thornton. (original Josephine Pullein Thompson character)

Ellie – older Blainstock Riding Stables student. She is a good rider and friend of Kirsty. She meets Jill in *Jill and the Mystery of the Missing Horse*.

Ellie Clutterbuck – one of two sisters who keep their ponies in the backgarden of their west Kensington home. They lead them out through the front door and ride around the streets of London and Hyde Park. Jill does a story about them for an article in *Horse and Hound*.

Elliott – Blainstock Riding Stables student, attends boarding school, shy, considered by the other students as 'posh'. He is eleven-years old in *All Change at Blainstock Stables*.

Mr Ellison-Heath – the husband of Evelyn Ellison-Heath and the father of Lavender, works for an insurance company in Oxford.

Em Sperrit – the sister of Ned Sperrit, the horse dealer. She lives with her brother in Preston, near Blackpool.

Ernest Shipton-Hill – a friend of Royce Pevensy, he is a poet who lives with his parents in a mansion near Birtle. At the time of the engagement party at Balinstock he is dating Serafina Collins. He is besotted with her and writes poems about her.

Etta (Henrietta Snook) – a Porlock Vale student, from Basinstoke.

Eugenia (Genie) – is an administrative assistant working on the film *Macbeth*.

Eustacia Pitt – a student at Porlock Vale, a clone of Susan Pyke.

Evelyn Ellison-Heath – mother of Lavender Ellison-Heath, godmother of Susan King (née Pyke), shares Mrs Pyke's passion for spiky hot-house plants. She is desperate to climb the social ladder and is befriended by Aggie Pevensy.

Evie – a modern young woman who works on the film *Macbeth*.

The Miss Farthingtons (Felicia and Jessica) – a pair of eccentric elderly sisters who keep a menagerie of animals in their large house, including Patchwork, a skewbald gelding which is stabled in the dining room.

Flora – an unprepossessing young woman with long, thin wispy hair and enormous spectacles. She is the assistant to the producer of the film *Macbeth*.

Florrie McIver – the youngest of the four McIver children whose parents run the general store in the small village near Blainstock Castle. She has black hair and loves ponies. She is eight-years old in *All Change at Blainstock Stables*.

Flossie Marlowe – lives at Thornhill, a friend of Richard Micheldever. They put Jill up for a night when she is travelling south to Cornwall to work for Bryony Peach.

Miss Follett – teaches veterinary care and stable management at Porlock Vale.

Foxy - Master of the Horse for the filming of *Macbeth* at Blainstock Castle. He is a ferrety little man, with slidey eyes and a twisted mouth and he doesn't like Jill.

Frank Stabley – a local showjumper from Chatton. He went to America to work for a horsey family. He returned with Yola and Jack Laskey, working as their horse trainer. They rented the Dower House at Blainstock for a 12 months. (original Ruby Ferguson character)

Mrs Frayne – the mother of Cassie Frayne a Blainstock Riding Stables student. She is searching for the perfect show pony to buy for her daughter.

Gary Horton – an up-and-coming showjumper who is engaged to April Cholly-Sawcutt, and running her father's showjumping yard.

George Pyke – a robust country gentleman, the father of Susan King, has a stable full of horses and enjoys going hunting with his cronies. (original Ruby Ferguson character)

Georgie (Georgina) Beeston – Porlock Vale student from Cheshire, who hopes to have her own riding school one day.

Gerry (Geraldine Royston) - Porlock Vale student from Texas who shares a room with Jill.

Gertrude Scobie – the wife of a landowner, Buster. Their farm is near Pevensy Park and they are good friends of Royce Pevensy.

Gwyneth Smith – a young woman with striking red hair and a strong Scottish accent, who stays at Blainstock Castle when the mare, Jewel, goes missing. In Book 5, Jill finds out that she is really the Countess of Waverton.

Hamish – Jill's younger half-brother whose mother is Catherine and father is Richard Micheldever.

Mr and Mrs Heath – the parents of the twins, Jackie and Val Heath. (original Ruby Ferguson characters)

Henry Talbot – married to Primrose Talbot, father of Cecilia, Jill's cousin.

Henry Thornton – nephew of Major Holbrooke, member of West Barsetshire Pony Club, almost a boyfriend of Noel Kettering (original Josephine Pullein Thompson character)

Henry Thurston – the local vet, competitor in point-to-points and hunter trials, boyfriend of Ann Derry.

Hermione Elliot – a beautiful actress who plays the part of Lady Macbeth when they filmed *Macbeth* at Blainstock Castle. She has a long pointy nose and hooked quivering nostrils, huge green eyes and thick voluptuous lips. She is also self-centred, vicious and malicious.

Hetty (Henrietta) Silverthorne – a young woman who is a journalist. She is going up to Scotland to get the inside track on Hermione Elliott and meets Jill on the train. Jill suggests that she get her into Blainstock to do her investigation and she pays Jill 'bed and board'.

Mrs Heyward – Australian woman who visited Blainstock Castle with her family. She has three children. They invite Jill to visit them in Australia and go showjumping on a circuit of the show up the east coast.

Mrs Higgins-Latham - one of the ladies at the dressage course at Porlock Vale that Jill attends.

Major Holbrooke – Chief Instructor of West Barsetshire Pony Club, uncle of Henry Thornton. He lives at Folly Court with his wife. (original Josephine Pullein Thompson character)

Horatio Lansdowne – the eldest son of Captain and Mrs Lansdowne. She is the sister of Richard Micheldever. Horatio is the elder brother of Mark Lansdowne.

Mrs Hipkiss – the chairman of the cottage hospital fund-raising committee.

Hugh Gillis – He was the stable manager at Blainstock Riding Stables, for many years, then becomes a part-owner of the business. He marries Linda McNally who brings her riding school ponies to Blainstock Stables, when she also became a part-owner of the stables business.

Jacinta – young Blainstock Riding Stables student, likeable, very pretty and average rider. She is thirteen-years old in *All Change at Blainstock Stables*.

Jack Laskey – a charming, handsome scoundrel who teaches riding at Porlock Vale Riding Centre. At one time, the object of Jill's infatuation. He becomes engaged to Willow Vetch. Later he turns up at Blainstock married to Yola.

Jackie Heath (Jacqueline Horrington-Hobday-Heath) – a lifelong friend of Ann and Jill, the twin sister of Val who goes to America working with horses. (original Ruby Ferguson character)

James Battleigh - local showjumper in Scotland.

James Bush – lifelong friend of Ann and Jill, brother of Diana, committed to point-to-pointing and steeplechasing. (original Ruby Ferguson character)

Janet Bulstrode – a famous three-day eventer. She works as a nurse and her sister Laura trains her horses in dressage.

Janet Fawley – young woman who grew up in Manchester and became a groom for the Claude family. She competes on the family's mare, Corrymeela and does well at a one-day event. She then goes on to a position with the Thorneycrofts. She goes to Blainstock Castle as a prize winner in a competition run by the magazine *Riding*. (original Diana Pullein Thompson character)

Jecca – great-niece of Bryony Peach, who inveigles Jill into a smuggling scheme in Cornwall.

Jill Crewe – the star of all the Jill books both by Ruby Ferguson and Jemma Spark. She spent her childhood living in Chatton, at Pool Cottage with her single mother, Catherine. When her mother married Richard Micheldever they move to Blainstock Castle in the Scottish Highlands. (original Ruby Ferguson character)

John – groom at Blainstock Castle, later becomes involved in the business, has a girlfriend, Arleen, who is an artist. He is a hard worker, good rider but has no equestrian ambitions to compete.

John Heyward – the second eldest boy of the three Australian Heyward children.

John Manners – member of West Barsetshire Pony Club, good friend of Susan Barington-Brown. (original Josephine Pullein Thompson character)

Joy Button – show secretary for the Kilkarny Gymkhana.

June Cholly-Sawcutt – the youngest of the three Cholly-Sawcutt sisters who are the daughters of Captain Cholly-Sawcutt. (original Ruby Ferguson character)

Jumbo – Blainstock Riding Stables student. He is overweight and is riding in order to lose weight. He is quite a good rider. He is fourteen-years old in *All Change at Blainstock Stables*.

Kirsty – older Blainstock Riding Stables student. She is a good rider and friend of Ellie. She has very curly black hair that sticks out at all angles and when she wears a riding cap. She meets Jill in *Jill and the Mystery of the Missing Horse*.

Kitty – the dressmaker who lives in the village near Blainstock Castle.

Captain Lansdowne – Mark Lansdowne's father, married to Lavinia, Richard Micheldever's sister. He owns the estate adjoining Blainstock Castle.

Laura Bulstrode – a famous show and dressage rider. She attends the Pevensy Christmas Party.

Lavender Ellison-Heath – an eleven-year-old girl with long brown hair, a small pixie face with a tip-tilted nose and unusual almond-shaped black eyes. She is the proud owner of Jill's pony Black Boy, attends a private day school in Birtle when Jill first meets her. She has two close friends, Morgan Pevensy and Ruby Swope.

Lavinia Lansdowne – wife of Captain Lansdowne, the sister of Richard Micheldever, mother of Horatio and Mark Lansdowne.

Lettie Lonsdale – young girl, buys Martini from Joan Penberthy and retrains her for pony club dressage and showjumping competitions. She goes to Blainstock Castle as a prize winner in a competition run by the magazine *Riding*. (original Diana Pullein Thompson character)

Lettie Tregarth – very good child rider recently arrived in Oxfordshire from Cornwall. She goes to Birtle Pony Club and becomes friends with Morgan Pevensy, Lavender Ellison-Heath and Ruby Swope.

Lily – a modern young woman who works on the film *Macbeth*.

Linda Gillis (née McNally) – owner of small riding school near the small village near Blainstock Riding Stables. She marries Hugh Gillis, who was the stable manager at Blainstock. They each become quarter owners in Blainstock Riding Stables, along with Jill and John. Linda has trained in dressage in Germany. She is a very good instructor and also a canny horse dealer.

Louis Pevensy - the Duke of Tolkington, the acquiescent husband of Aggie, father of five children, he has a passion for motor cars.

Louisa – very young Blainstock Riding Stables student, beginner rider. She is ten years old in *All Change at Blainstock Stables*.

Maddie – the best Blainstock Stables riding student, smart, likeable, best friends with Vera. She is fifteen-years old in *All Change at Blainstock Stables*.

Maggie McIver – the second of the four McIver children whose parents run the general store in the small village near Blainstock Castle. She has bright red hair and loves ponies. She is fourteen-years old in *All Change at Blainstock Stables*.

Mark – he is a twin brother of Ned. They live in the Scottish Highlands in a far-flung croft, speak with thick accents and have unkempt hair, scruffy jumpers and laced riding boots. They ride at Blainstock Riding Stables in *All Change at Blainstock Stables.*=-

Martin Lowe – a middle-aged man in a wheelchair who taught Jill to ride when she had first bought Black Boy. (original Ruby Ferguson character)

Mathew Solent – drop-dead gorgeous actor who plays the part of Macbeth during the filming at Blainstock. He has coppery curly hair and wonderful blue eyes and a mellow baritone voice. Jill and her mother are entranced with him when he arrives at the castle.

May Cholly-Sawcutt – the middle one of the three Cholly-Sawcutt sisters who are the daughters of Captain Cholly-Sawcutt. (original Ruby Ferguson character)

Mr and Mrs McNally – the parents of Linda Gillis (née McNally). They are Christian missionaries based in Africa.

The Honourable Mercedes Pevensy – the eldest daughter of Aggie and Louis, a remote, classically beautiful young woman. She is a very good rider with a serious and conscientious character. She rides successfully in three-day events.

Mercy Dulbottle – gawky, awkward young woman who knew Jill as a child and is now involved in CND. (original Ruby Ferguson character)

Mrs Merrivale – the farmer wife of a family who live on Dartmoor.

Mr Merrivale – the father of the Merrivale family who live on a farm at Dartmoor.

Mick - a Birmingham boy who comes up to work at Linda's riding school with his friend Scott one summer when the mare Jewel goes missing.

Mrs Milner – the Pevensy Cook.

The Honourable Morgan Pevensy – an eleven-year-old girl, the youngest of the five Pevensy children. She is friends with Lavender Ellison-Heath and Ruby Swope. She is not much interested in horse riding and is a very good artist.

Ned - he is a twin brother of Mark. They live in the Scottish Highlands in a far-flung croft, speak with thick accents and have unkempt hair, scruffy jumpers and laced riding boots. They ride at Blainstock Riding Stables in *All Change at Blainstock Stables.*

Ned Sperrit – a horse dealer, friend of Richard Micheldever, lives in Preston. Jill buys Copperplate from him.

Noel Kettering – Susan Barington-Brown's best friend, member of West Barsetshire Pony Club. She broke in and trained Tranquil, who is sold to Susan. (original Josephine Pullein Thompson character)

Noel Lemming – runs a jump racing stable in Oxfordshire.

Norah Heywood – the youngest of the three Australian Heywood children. She becomes involved with an undesirable young man and her mother invites Jill to visit them, hoping this will help the situation.

Norrie Cannon - one of the Australian twins who has 'riding lessons' from Jill Crewe when they are visiting one of their relatives in England. (original Ruby Ferguson character)

Ophelia Nettlebed – young woman who was the former owner of Copperplate.

Olly Merrivale – teenage boy, eldest of the five Merrivale children who live on a farm in Dartmoor.

Oswald Tettington-Ford – a Porlock Vale student who was called Blubberbox at school, from Gloucestershire, studying to give riding lessons at his family's livery stable.

Pablo Rodriguez Camellia – a student at Porlock Vale from Spain.

Pat Clutterbuck – one of two sisters who keep their ponies in the backgarden of their west Kensington home. They lead them out through the front door and ride around the streets of London and Hyde Park. Jill does a story about them for an article in *Horse and Hound*.

Patrick Huntingdon – a young man, who with his sister Sara, owns a pony, called Adonis. He has grown out of the pony and borrows his friend Val's horse, Scarlet Pimpernel. He goes to Blainstock Castle as a prize winner in a competition run by the magazine *Riding*. (original Josephine Pullein Thompson character)

Miss Penwith – retired Pevensy nanny.

Perry – older Blainstock Riding Stables student. He is very shy and quite good rider. He is sixteen-years old in *All Change at Blainstock Stables*.

Mrs Phyllis Whirtley – lives at Blossom Park, where various horse events are held. She helps Dinah Dean and arranges for her to go to boarding school. (original Ruby Ferguson character)

Pierre – a young French aristrocrat, with whom Ann Derry became infatuated.

Miss Pomfret – judge of riding classes at Chatton Show in 1963, reputed to always prefer chestnuts and won't look at blacks.

Poppet – a modern young woman who works on the film *Macbeth*.

The Honourable Porsche Pevensy – a seventeen-year-old young woman, the fourth of the five Pevensy children, a wild child, a very good rider and desperately ambitious, suffers from crushing sibling rivalry with her older sister, Mercedes. She and her brother, Austin, often make mischief together.

Posy Merrivale – one of five Merrivale children who live on a farm in Dartmoor.

Primrose Talbot – mother of Cecilia, sister of Catherine, Jill's mother, married to Henry, lives at White Ferry (original Ruby Ferguson character)

Priscilla – young woman the same age as Jill who lives in Chatton, in a large ugly house called Abbey Mansions. She had an ugly pony and boasted about him, and he bucked her off in front of Jill and Ann.

Mrs Pyke – wife of George, mother of Susan, best friends with Evelyn Ellison-Heath, loves spiky hothouse flowers. (original Ruby Ferguson character).

Reg – a friend of Willow Vetch. He has pale skin and freckles, with curly dark hair and blue eyes

Robbie Heyward – the eldest of the three Australian Heyward children.

Roman Marlowe – lives in Thornhill, a friend of Richard Micheldever. Jill stays with him and his wife when she is travelling south to Cornwall to work for Bryony Peach.

Rosie Merrivale – one of the five Merrivale children who live on a farm at Dartmoor.

Rennie Jordan – young woman who suffered psychological trauma as a child. She is rehabilitated through riding horses and goes to Miss Brandon's riding stable and learns to ride. She goes to Blainstock Castle as a prize winner in a competition run by the magazine *Riding*. (original Monica Dickens character)

Richard Micheldever – the owner of Blainstock Castle who marries Catherine, the mother of Jill Crewe.

Captain Romanski – elegant, lean, elegant, Polish riding instructor at Porlock Vale.

The Honourable Royce Pevensy – the eldest Pevensy child, who will inherit the title and be a Duke when his father dies. He writes poetry, likes riding but concentrates on managing the Pevensy Park estate.

Ruby Swope – young girl who is a helper at Mrs Darcy's riding school, lives in Ditching Hollow in a caravan. She is a very enthusiastic young horsewoman, not backwards in coming forwards. She is friends with Morgan Pevensy and Lavender Ellison-Heath.

Rupert – an upper-class young man who is friends with Amanda Applewood.

Ruth – working pupil at Porlock Vale.

Lady Rutherford-Flint - one of the ladies at the dressage course at Porlock Vale that Jill attends.

Sandy Merrivale – second girl in the Merrivale family of five children. They live on a farm on Dartmoor.

Scott – a Birmingham boy with large freckles on his squashy nose. Comes up to work at Linda's riding school with his friend Mick one summer when the mare Jewel goes missing.

Serafina Collins – a very delicate, china doll beauty who attends the Pevensy Chrismas Party and entrances all the men including Royce Pevensy. She is the girlfriend of Royce's best friend when she attends the engagement party at Blainstock.

Serena – the riding instructor at Mrs Darcy's riding school.

Serena Colchester – does the catering for Catherine's, Jill Crewe's mother, for her wedding to Richard Micheldever.

Sheila – young Blainstock Riding Stables student. She is bright as a button, a beginner rider. She is nine-years old in *All Change at Blainstock Stables*.

Simon Caxton-Thorpe – tall, slim young man with pale skin and Irish black hair, a poet, good friends with Royce Pevensy, lives at home in his parents' home, a mansion near Birtle. His girlfriend is Dinah Dean.

Mrs Southgate-de Long – one of the ladies on the one-week dressage course at Porlock Vale which Jill attends in *Jill and the Horsemasters*.

Miss Square – an elderly woman who lives in the village near Blainstock Castle. She gives Jill Crewe lessons in shorthand and German.

Captain Stefinski – He is the proprietor of the Surrey riding school where Sara and Patrick Huntingdon learned to ride, and where Adonis, their pony is stabled. (original Josephine Pullein Thompson character)

Stewart McIver – the third of the four McIver children whose parents run the general store in the small village near Blainstock Castle. He has red hair and loves ponies. He is ten-years old in *All Change at Blainstock Stables*.

Mr and Mrs Street – the parents of Clarabell, who purchased Black Boy from one of Ruby Swope's unscrupulous relatives, Billy Dudgeon.

Susan Barington-Brown – a young woman who has been a member of the West Barsetshire Pony Club for many years. She is best friends with Noel Kettering. She goes to Blainstock Castle as a prize winner in a competition run by the magazine *Riding*. (original Josephine Pullein Thompson character)

Susan King (née Pyke) – Jill's rival throughout her child hood years. She would openly scoff at Jill when she was first learning to ride and hung around with a crew of like-minded girls who followed her lead. She married Bartholomew King, a local solicitor, and lives in a new house in a development on the outskirts of Rychester. Is a close friend of Austin and Porsche Pevensy. (original Ruby Ferguson character)

The Honourable Sylvia Latchington-Field – young horsewoman who is competing in dressage in Devon, she is thinking of going in for eventing. She meets Jill who is competing in a dressage event on Balius.

Tanya – half Russian, half English, a young woman who owns a pretty hunter called Minuet, who is friends with Janet Fawley.

Tartine – a very elegant French woman who lives in London and is friends with Ann Derry.

Tatiana de Vere– proprietor at the 'De Luxe Movie Stables'.

Ted - a young boy with bright red hair and large freckles across his snub nose who rides at Mrs Darcy's riding school.

Colonel Ted Motley – a retired horseman who has recently moved to Chatton and is on the organising committee of Chatton Show. He becomes close to Mrs Darcy.

Lady Telford-Talbot – one of the ladies at the dressage course at Porlock Vale that Jill attends.

Mrs Templeton-Watters - one of the ladies at the dressage course at Porlock Vale that Jill attends.

Thea – member of the Birtle Pony Club, friend of Morgan Pevensy.

Theodore Chapman – a friend of Royce Pevensy, he attends the engagement party at Blainstock. He is very attractive with blonde hair and blue eyes, a Scandinavian look.

Mrs Thornton – the mother of Henry Thornton. She is a tall, rather solid woman, with long grey hair worn in a loose knot at the nape of her neck. She talks a lot, asking questions and doesn't wait for answers. (original Josephine Pullein Thompson character)

Mr Titchley – Manager of Goddards Department Store, who donated the prizes to the Blossom Park Hunter Trials.

Tom – a groom at Pevensy Park stables, devoted to Porsche.

Tommy – very young Blainstock Riding Stables student, still on the lead rein. He is five-years old in *All Change at Blainstock Stables.*

Val Heath (Valeria Horrington-Hobday-Heath) – twin sister of Jackie Heath, lifelong friend of Jill Crewe, goes to America to work as a riding instructor at the same time as Frank Stabley. (original Ruby Ferguson character)

Valentine Scroops - Hunt Secretary of Tip Top Hunt, lives at Nutwith House, Beadle.

Valerie Barington-Brown – elder sister of Susan Barington-Brown, very interested in home decoration schemes. (original Josephine Pullein Thompson character)

Mr Vail – a farmer who lives on Dartmoor, a friend of Mr Merrivale.

Venetia Delphinton – lives near Cheltenham, a glamorous woman, wife of Charles Delphinton, a racehorse trainer. They're friends of Richard Micheldever. Jill stays with them when she is travelling south to work for Bryony Peach.

Vera – older Blainstock Riding Stables rider, good rider, best friend of Maddie. She is sixteen years old in *All Change at Blainstock Stables.*

Violet – a young girl who usually rides Blackstone at Mrs Darcy's riding school.

Walters children – three children who live in the Vicarage, who have a pony called Ballerina. They set up a riding stable with Jill Crewe when she is spending time staying at her cousin Cecilia's house, White Ferry. (original Ruby Ferguson characters)

Wendy Mead – a lifelong friend of Jill and Ann, runs Mrs Darcy's riding school when she is away, hopes to become the proprietor when Mrs Darcy retires. (original Ruby Ferguson character)

Colonel Whetton – instructor at Porlock Vale.

Willow Vetch – the daughter of Bernard Vetch, an American arms dealer. A strange looking girl with an egg-shaped head. She attended the Porlock Vale horsemasters course and became engaged to Jack Laskey.

Yola Laskey – a young American heiress who marries Jack Laskey. They leave America in disgrace as Jack has thrown over his fiancée, Willow Vetch, and rent the Dower House at Blainstock Stables for a year.

Yvonne Dufour – a friend of Ann Derry, who lives in Paris.

ANIMALS

Adonis – grey Anglo-Arab pony, 14.2 hh, used to belong to the Merrimans who were persuaded that he was a rogue. He was ridden secretly by Patrick and Sara Huntingdon when they were staying with the Merrimans, who then gave him to Patrick and Sara. Patrick grew out of him and Sara rides him. He is on livery at Captain Stefinski stables in Surrey. (original Josephine Pullein Thompson character)

Archer – thickset cob, 16.2 hh, three-day eventer, good at jumping but needs more dressage training, owned by Mark Lansdowne who leases him to Patrick Huntingdon who is one of the prize winners who spends two weeks at Blainstock.

Ballerina – the pony who belongs to the Walters children who started up a riding stable with Jill Crewe in *Jill Has a Stable*. (original Ruby Ferguson character)

Balius – grey gelding, 16.1 hh, three-quarter thoroughbred, one quarter Highland pony. Son of Bonnie, full-brother to Shadow. Given to Jill Crewe by her step-father when she first goes to live at Blainstock Castle.

Banjo – beautiful bay gelding, owned by Mercedes Pevensy, her best horse and prospective mount for Burghley and Badminton, died after a bad fall when ridden recklessly by Porsche Pevensy.

Banjo – Porlock Vale horse assigned to Geraldine Royston.

Beauty – beautiful show pony owned by Susan Barington-Brown when she was young. Later sold to Nicholas and Jonathan Lucien. (original Josephine Pullein Thompson character)

Bill – beautiful bay gelding, 15.3 hh, a white star and two white foreleg socks, ex-racehorse owned by Linda Gillis (née McNally).

Black Boy – black pony gelding, 13.2 hh, the most famous pony in the world of Jill, her first pony. He is then sold on to Lavender Ellison-Heath, who for a time renamed him Bingle Jells but then reverted to his original name. Jill manages to buy him later and he goes to live at Blainstock Stables. (Ruby Ferguson character)

Black Comedy – ex-steeplechaser, big brown horse with a rectangular head and thick, scarred legs, previously owned by Jill Crewe who rescued him from a horrid, cruel man. Jill later sold him to Ann Derry, who likes to hack him around lanes.

Blackstone – small black pony at Mrs Darcy's riding school.

Bonnie – an aged mare, 15.1 hh, half Highland pony and half thoroughbred. She is trained as a harness horse and sometimes pulls the trap. She is also a very able cross-country jumper. Jill Crewe rides her when she first goes to live a Blainstock Castle. She is the dam of Shadow and Balius.

British Brown – tall, lightly-built brown thoroughbred, one of Mark Lansdowne's three-day eventers that he has competed on at Burghley Three-Day Event.

Brownie – brown gelding, cob, owned by Richard Micheldever. He is used as a pack horse during the shooting season and also as a riding horse in the Blainstock Riding Stables.

Brownie – one of three light-boned Arab geldings: brown with a dished head and dainty muzzle ridden by one of the three witches when they filmed *Macbeth* at Blainstock Castle.

Bright Eyes – home-bred bay gelding owned by Wendy Mead, entered in the novice horse event at Blossom Park Hunter Trials.

Cammie – 14.2 hh, placid chestnut gelding, one of the Blainstock Riding Stable horses.

Carousel- the horse assigned to Georgie Beeston at Porlock Vale. He is 16 hh, huge hindquarters, a broad chest, a prominent Roman nose with wide-blown nostrils and a devilish personality, prone to spasmodie bucking fits.

Christie – pale, palomino pony owned by Angela, who is a member of Birtle Pony Club in Oxfordshire.

Chunk – a plain, sensible, chunky cob, one of Mrs Darcy's riding school horses.

Cinnamon - large raw-boned Thoroughbred mare, off the track and re-trained by Linda Gillis (née McNally).

Copperplate – chestnut Arab mare, 15.3 hh, distinctive markings include a splash of white on her belly, crooked white blaze and four white socks. Ned Sperrit sold her to Jill as an experienced showjumper.

Cornish Boy – workmanlike hunter-type pony that wins many hunter trials, owned by Lettie Tregarth who has moved from Cornwall to Oxfordshire and has joined the Birtle Pony Club.

Dauntless – chestnut gelding owned by Henry Thurston, who competes in hunter trials and National Hunt races.

Delight – colt foal of Copperplate. He has an unusual curly coat.

Diablo – an evil black gelding with a malevolent nature but fast and fearless over jumps, owned by George Pyke, ridden by Susan King (née Pyke), entered in the open event at Blossom Park Hunter Trials. Porsche Pevensy later arranges for him to be swapped with Sassy Swoop.

Dragon – Porlock Vale horse assigned to Bob Nutley. He is a solid, plain and unimaginative animal.

Dumpty – fantastic gymkhana pony, Thea's previous pony before he was traded in for a show pony, Summer Fancy.

Evening Echo – bay thoroughbred gelding owned by Henry Thornton. (original Josephine Pullein Thompson characer)

Firefly – good looking chestnut gelding with four white socks and a white diamond on his forehead, owned and ridden by Austin Pevensy and entered in the open event at Blossom Park Horse Trials.

Firestorm – huge, impressive chestnut gelding, over 17 hh. Originally owned by Mark Lansdowne, then Blainstock Stables, later sold to Jack Laskey.

Golden Wonder – beautiful show pony, originally owned by June Creswell, an annoying show rider who is a member of West Barsetshire Pony Club. Later sold to Susan Barington-Brown. When Susan grows out of Golden Wonder and Beauty they are sold to Nicholas and Jonathan Lucien. (original Josephine Pullein Thompson character)

Goldie – foal of Jewel, the mare who disappeared from Blainstock, which belonged to Gwyneth Smith, aka the Countess of Waverton.

Harlequin – mare, dark brown with splashy white blaze and three white stockings. She has a large head with a Roman nose, and a placid temperament. Her grand-sire was Rocket, the Dartmoor stallion who runs on the moor and her grand-dam was a tall, rather spindly Thoroughbred mare. These two had produced a mare who was bred to a Gipsy Cob who produced Harlequin. She is owned by the Merrivale family.

Hector – Porlock Vale horse assigned to Dieter Schunker. He is piebald horse with blue eyes, and a mane which is half black and half white.

Irish Boy – grey thoroughbred, owned by James Bush, entered in the novice event at Blossom Park Hunter Trials.

Jack – an ex-racehorse bought by Linda Gillis (née McNally) to retrain.

Jackdaw - over 15 hh, his grand-sire was Rocket, the Dartmoor stallion who runs on the moor and his grand-dam was a tall, rather spindly Thoroughbred mare. These two had produced a mare who was bred to an Arab stallion who produced Jackdaw.

Jago – big, bay, wild thoroughbred, owned by James Bush, entered in the open event at Blossom Park Hunter Trials.

Joe (racing name Charles Chumly) – big thoroughbred gelding, ex-racehorse, a little ewe-necked and goose-rumped, he is being retrained by Linda Gillis, when she was Linda McNally and running her own riding school.

Jester – 15 hh gelding, one of the Blainstock Riding Stables horses.

Jewel – a cremello mare who is stabled at Blainstock when she disappears. She later produces a golden-coloured colt with curly hair, called Goldie.

Killmousky – smoky grey cat belongs to Blainstock Castle's Cook, an extremely good mouse catcher.

Kilkarny King – three-day eventer owned by Mark Lasdowne.

King – a huge horse with Clydesdale breeding, bright golden chestnut with a broad white blaze and four white socks, ridden by the King in the film *Macbeth*, when it was filmed at Blainstock Castle.

La Blonde – showy show pony owned by Susan Pyke when she and Jill were young teenagers. (original Ruby Ferguson character)

Lancaster Bomber – jumper owned by James Bush, entered in the novice event at Blossom Park Hunter Trials to be ridden by James' sister, Diana.

Mangala – ungainly grey gelding, ex-racehorse bought at a sale by the Pevensys, with a view to retraining him for cross-country and eventing. Ridden by Porsche at the Blossom Park Hunter Trials.

Martini – bay mare, 14.2 hh, out of pony hunter, Sherry, by Rascal of Rapallo. Broken in by her owner Guy Beaumont, then sold to Pip Cox who is very nervous and gets run away with in the hunting field. Sold to Lydia Pike who abuses her and is humiliated when she is run away with at Stringwell Show. Sold at auction to Lettie Londsdale.

Midge – a merry little grey pony, a mount for Fleance when they filmed *Macbeth* at Blainstock.

Minuet - dark bay mare, 15.1 hh, with a finely cut head and large eyes. Belongs to Tanya, who is a friend of Janet Fawley.

Misty – one of three light-boned Arab geldings, with a dished head and dainty muzzle which were ridden by the three witches when *Macbeth* was filmed at Blainstock Castle.

Misty – grey Highland pony, 13 hh, lively and very good at gymkhana games, one of the Blainstock Riding Stables ponies.

Mouse – a huge, magnificent, rampaging, chestnut gelding, with a wide chest and flaring, snorting nostrils. He is the mount for *Macbeth* when they are filming at Blainstock Castle.

Mousie – a small, dun pony mare at Mrs Darcy's riding school.

Ned – an ex-racehorse who is bought by Linda Gillis (née McNally) to be re-trained.

Old Nick – black gelding owned by Linda Gillis

Oriole - 12 hh, plain brown, ill-tempered and stubborn pony who is one of the Blainstock Riding Stables ponies.

Patchwork – skewbald gelding belonging to the Miss Farthingtons, stabled in their dining room while he is being trained as an eventer. Initially, it was Serena, the riding instructor at Mrs Darcy's who trained him. Then Mark Lansdowne went to stay with the Farthingtons and he took over.

Peppie (short for Pepper) - 14.1 hh, blue-roan with an ugly square head, brilliant at jumping, one of the Blainstock Riding Sables ponies.

Popcorn – jumping horse ridden by Gary Horton in a novice event at the Blossom Park Hunter Trials.

Prince – 14.3hh grey Welsh pony, very quiet and lazy, one of the Blainstock Riding Stables ponies.

Puzzle – a pretty little skewbald mare who was trained by Linda for clients. She appeared in *Jill and the Mystery of the Missing Horse*.

Rapide – bay, 14.2 hh gelding, the second most famous pony in the world of Jill. He was her showjumper, full of character and mischievous quirks, was being ridden by Porsche Pevensy last season but now is assigned to the youngest Pevensy child, Morgan, who likes him but isn't keen on riding in general. (original Ruby Ferguson character)

Rat – a thickset chestnut cob, the mount for Banquo when they filmed *Macbeth* at Blainstock Castle.

Red – one of three light-boned Arab geldings, with a dished head and dainty muzzle, ridden by the three witches when they filmed *Macbeth* at Blainstock Castle.

Red Hornet – chestnut steeplechaser gelding, 17.2 hh owned by Gary Horton and April Cholly-Sawcutt, entered in the open event at Blossom Park Hunter Trials in *Jill and the Steeplechaser*.

Red Moontrader – beautiful 16 hh chestnut gelding, which is being trained at Mrs Darcy's riding school in Chatton. Jill rides him in *Jill Rides Cross-Country*.

Rex - pretty Welsh pony, 12.2 hh. He mainly trots and rarely canters, one of the Blainstock Riding Stables ponies. He always wins the trotting races.

Rocket - dark brown Dartmoor stallion that runs up on the moor near the Merrivales' farm. He has sired many of their ponies, some of whom who have then been bred to other horses.

Rosy –sweet-tempered red roan mare assigned to Etta at Porlock Vale.

Sassy Swoop –glamourous and sparkling mare with large dark eyes and perfectly shaped pointed ears, owned by the Pevensys. Later swapped for Diablo and becomes the property of Susan King (née Pyke).

Sausage Roll – the horse assigned to Jill at Porlock Vale when she studies to be a riding instructor. He is a solid, plain brown cob with a thick neck and a scruffy mane.

Scarlet Pimpernel – tall gelding with long legs and long ears, belongs to Valerie, who lends him to her friend Patrick Huntingdon to ride. He takes him to Blainstock Castle when he goes there as a prize winner in a competition run by the magazine *Riding*.

Secret – grey anglo-arab mare, 15.1 hh purchased from Claire by Charles Ravenscroft who trains her as a showjumper. (original Josephine Pullein Thompson character)

Shadow – grey gelding, 16 hh, three-quarter thoroughbred, one quarter Highland pony, Son of Bonnie, full-brother to Balius. He was traded by Mark Lansdowne to Blainstock Riding Stables as part of a deal.

Sherpa – Scottish deerhound belongs to Richard Micheldever.

Sirius – tall, brown and serious gelding, with no mischievous twists and turns in his character, owned by Mercedes Pevensey, one of her eventers, reliable but unlikely to be a champion, entered in the open class at Blossom Park Hunter Trials.

Skydiver – utterly gorgeous grey gelding, highly-trained in dressage and owned by Jill Crewe, later sold to Yola Laskey.

Spirit Dancer – the horse assigned to Ariel Bergman when she is a student at Porlock Vale. He is a silver grey, with a heart-breakingly beautiful Arab head, huge liquid eyes, and neat, curved ears.

Star - 11 hh, a lead rein pony who is one of the Blainstock Riding Stables ponies.

Summer Fancy – pretty, bay pony with black legs, perfect head with a broad forehead and a tiny white star, small, neat ears and large soulful eyes. Thea's show pony destined for Harringay, then sold to Lavender Ellison-Heath whose mother wants her to have a top notch show pony.

Sunset – Porlock Vale horse assigned to Angela Cartwright, prone to kicking other horses.

Tabitha – Porlock Vale mare assigned to Willow Vetch. She is a scrawny, flea-bitten grey, full of fads and crotchets.

Taffy - dun mare, 13 hh, the colour of caramel and ill-tempered, one of the Blainstock Riding Stables ponies.

Tippy – 14.1 hh, a very pretty aged mare with a pretty dished face, who is one of the Blainstock Riding Stables ponies and has been leased to the four McIver children for their exclusive use but still stabled at Blainstock.

Totty – retired small grey gelding who served his time in Mrs Darcy's riding school for many years. Ann Derry borrows him so that Black Comedy has some company at Pool Cottage.

Tranquil – bay anglo-arab 15.1 hh gelding. He was trained by Noel Kettering and is then sold to Susan Barington-Brown who goes to Blainstock Castle as a prize winner in a competition run by the magazine *Riding*. (original Josephine Pullein Thompson character)

Treasure – Porlock Vale horse assigned to Pablo Rodriguez Camellia. He is a good-lokingul bay gelding, with long, slender legs, an elegant neck, a noble head and very alert, intelligent ears.

Troubadour – faithful old hunter belonging to the Pevensys. Morgan rides him to a Birtle Pony Club rally.

Turpin - 15.2 hh, brown and plain, rescued from pulling a cart in Glasgow, one of the Blainstock Riding Stables horses.

Twillen - 16.3 hh, rather plain brown thoroughbred three-day eventer owned by Mark Lansdowne and kept on livery at Blainstock Riding Stables.

Twinkle - small pony belonging to Buttons Merrivale, who lives on a farm in Dartmoor.

Wycombe – a Porlock Vale horse assigned to Oswald Tettington-Ford.

What was happening in 1964?

The 1960s were the epoch when the 'permissive society' was born. The contraceptive pill, psychobabble, and sex were all on the agenda. Hemlines were going up, inhibitions were coming down, and the Beatles were all the rage. The lace curtains were being drawn back. The Cold War was raging, and there were a plethora of spies on both sides of the Iron Curtain. Guy Burgess, Donald Maclean and Kim Philby were in the news, and the Duke of Windsor's Nazi sympathies became known.

J F Kennedy was assassinated in June 1963, and his successor, a democrat, President Lyndon B Johnson, pushed the Civil Rights Act through in February 1964. This meant that discrimination based on race, colour, religion, sex and ethnic origins became illegal in America. The Beatles had a 1964 UK tour and then a world tour and were greeted with hysterical enthusiasm.

In geopolitical terms, many African countries were in the process of seeking and gaining independence – in 1961, Tanganyika and Sierra Leone; 1962 Uganda; in 1963, Kenya and Zanzibar; 1964, Nyasaland, which was renamed Malawi, and Northern Rhodesia became Zambia; and in 1965, the Gambia. With the Cold War at its height in these years, both the United States and the Soviet Union were active in many African countries.

The cosy, innocent, pony-loving world of the 1950s, in which the Pullein Thompson sisters and Ruby Ferguson penned their classic pony books, was moving on. Writing Jill Crewe's story as she becomes an adult in the 1960s is a challenge. In my books, Jill turns twenty-one in August 1964. The charm of Jill's robust innocence was one of the qualities that Ruby

Ferguson's readers loved. However, in terms of historical fiction, which is what the Jill books have become, one cannot entirely ignore the social context in which Jill is living as she grows older. I have tried to balance Jill's horse-centric existence with the character of Dinah Dean, who has become involved in social issues. Then, there is the tricky issue of Jill moving into a relationship that may lead to marriage. Ann Derry is unofficially engaged to her boyfriend, the vet Henry Thurston. In contrast, Jill has remained resolutely single.

Although some aspects of life in the UK were changing, equestrian sports were as popular as ever. Horse riding became accessible to more ordinary people, not just the gentry and landowners.

Badminton in 1964 was a big event as it was the run-up to the Tokyo Olympics held in October. Major General James Templer won it on M'Lord Connelly, a 16.2 hh anglo-arab. This pair had come second at Little Badminton in 1962. Controversially, they had not competed in any previous events during the winter of 1963-1964 and went straight to Badminton. This made them unpopular with the pundits who felt that they should have been competing during the winter in the run-up to Badminton. M'Lord Connelly could be a brilliant horse, but he also had a nasty 'stop' in him, and you could never be sure when he might put in a refusal. At Badminton that year, he gained maximum bonus points around the steeplechase and the fastest time in the cross-country. James Templer did as he always did and ran beside his horse around the Roads and Tracks in order to save his mount's energy. It was in the time before the course was roped, and he always took the straightest line between the fences. J. D. Smith-Bingham riding By Golly came second, and the Irish Olympic rider, Tony Cameron, riding Black Salmon came third. Sheila Waddington (née Willcox) won Little Badminton on Glenamoy.

Horses travelling to the Tokyo Olympics were flown in by air. If a horse became uncontrollable in the air, they had to be destroyed. This happened to the US eventer, Markam, and an Argentinian horse which was put down on the return flight. A Chilean horse died of a heart attack while flying.

The showjumping course was formidable. There were 46 riders from 17 nations. The most difficult jump was towards the end of the course, a 5-metre wide water jump, followed by a left turn to a very large oxer. Only six riders cleared the water in both rounds, and only three cleared it and the final oxer without faults. The French rider, Pierre Jonquères d'Oriola, won the gold on Lutteur B. The German rider, Hermann Schridde, won the silver on Dozent II, and the British rider Peter Robeson won the bronze on Firecrest. In the team showjumping competition, the gold went to the German team, the silver to the French team and the bronze to the Italians.

Peter Robeson had previously won a bronze medal in the team showjumping event in the Australian Olympics in 1956. His best horses included Craven A, Firecrest, and Grebe. He was married to Rene, an heiress to the Rothschild dynasty and together, they ran a small yard of homebred National Hunt racehorses. Peter was known for his dry sense of humour and no-nonsense style. He died in 2018.

Only six countries had sufficient rider and horse combinations to enter the dressage team competition: Germany, Switzerland, Sweden, Japan, the

Soviet Union and the USA. In those days, dressage was not big in Britain. In the individual dressage event, the Swiss rider, Henri Chammartin, won gold on Wörmann, the German rider Harry Boldt, won silver on Remus, and the Soviet Union, Sergio Filotov, won the bronze on Absent. In the team dressage event, the Germans won gold, the Swiss won silver, and the Soviet Union won the bronze.

The three-day event competition consisted of a 31-obstacle cross-country course which was considered too straightforward for Olympic standards. In the individual competition, Italian rider Mauro Checcoli won gold on Sunbeam. The Argentinian rider Carlos Moratorio won silver on Chalan, and the German rider Fritz Ligges won bronze on Donkosak. In the team eventing competition, the Italian team won the gold, the United States team won the silver, and the bronze went to the German team.

James Templer on M'Lord Connelly was in the British team after a fantastic win at Badminton that year. They were fourth after the dressage but eliminated on the cross-country when M'Lord Connelly refused the third jump from the finish.

Jill and the Mystery of the Missing Horse

Part I

In the summer of 1962, the Glorious Twelfth came with a burst of bright golden sunshine, lighting up the purple ling and heralding another Scottish summer. But don't mention the midges! Just in case, you're not *au fait* with the concept of the Glorious Twelfth it is the twelfth of August and marks the first day of the grouse shooting season. On this day, more grouse are shot than on any other day.

For us at Blainstock Castle, it marks the beginning of the busiest time of the year. Cars full of shooters who come for just this day descend on us. Then we have those who stay a week or two, in a more leisurely pursuit of recreation, a little shooting, and an experience of the Highlands.

Mummy and her husband, Richard and I are up to our necks in work; making our house guests comfortable and providing them with the best shooting, delicious meals, and a hefty dose of Scottish tradition. For those who choose not to shoot they can walk around the estate and up into the hills, sail on the loch or go down to Linda McNally's riding school for a day's trekking. For our guests, it is the most idyllic holiday. For us, it is our bread and butter, and we have hardly a moment to catch our breaths.

We were sitting down to a sumptuous dinner in the long dining room on perhaps the sixteenth of August, I cannot remember the exact date, when one of the guests asked Richard for how many generations had his family lived at the castle. I saw that my stepfather was just a little discomfited, he had to admit that in fact, his family were relatively *parvenu*.

"We came to live in the castle in about 1875, nearly ninety years ago, when my grandfather took possession," he had replied blandly.

"So, it wasn't really your ancestral home?" pressed the guest.

"No, previously it had belonged to the MacTaggarts, who had lived here for many generations, stretching back into the Scottish mists of time," replied Richard in a vague attempt at lyricism.

"Are there any MacTaggarts left in the area?" asked the guest mildly.

"No, I believe they moved to Edinburgh. We really haven't kept in contact," replied Richard, perhaps a little sheepishly. Although how the events of ninety years ago pertained to him were not clear.

"Actually, my mother was a MacTaggart, and I do believe that the man who lost Blainstock was my great-great-uncle. Your grandfather won the castle from him in a game of cards."

"Really!" exclaimed Richard. I sat there dumbfounded. It was like one of those gorgeous mysteries set in castles where the descendants of an ancient family have been cheated out of their inheritance and return to wreak their vengeance.

Up until now, this guest had been rather overlooked. He was a very quietly spoken older man, a bachelor who had come to walk the Scottish hills and look at the sky, taking a break from the crowded streets of Edinburgh. He had no desire to shoot grouse, and when he wasn't outside breathing the bracing fresh air, he spent his time in the library, perusing old books. Today he was dressed in very mundane clothes, a pair of brown slacks and matching brogues and a very 'accountantish' cardigan of blue and green. Obviously, his mother had not raised him with the stricture that 'blue and green should never be seen'.

My imagination took off at a gallop, and I wondered if he had come here to spy out the land and make a bid to reclaim his rightful inheritance. It was as if he read my mind.

"Don't worry, I am merely curious, I have no desire to avenge the honour of my family," he said looking directly at me. "My great-great-uncle was from all accounts a very foolish man prone to gambling and wenching and deserved to lose the estate. I'm happy to see that it is in good order and well-lived in."

These were reassuring words, although I was rather intrigued with the idea of 'wenching', which I knew meant associating with Loose Women. But then, I thought suspiciously, if he had come to Wreak Vengeance then this was the sort of thing he would say. He would hardly reveal his dastardly plan over the dinner table. Perhaps this was a Machiavellian strategy to lull us into a false sense of security.

The next morning the man, who was called Arthur Branson set off with a stout walking stick, heading towards the loch, taking with him a picnic lunch. I watched him from one of the castle windows as I attacked each of the guests' beds, attempting hospital corners, dusting, sweeping and flinging open windows to let in the sweet Highland air. Mummy had insisted that I do only half the rooms today as she had some girls coming up from the village and I was to be given most of the day off to take my grey gelding, Balius down to Linda's riding school to go out with her and some clients on a ride. Two of the guests from the castle were also riding

today, so I was still 'on duty' so to speak.

The horse-riders were two young women, perhaps a few years older than me, who had arrived several days ago. They were both tall and athletic; Gwyneth had striking red hair and a strong Scottish accent, obviously Celtic to the bone; the other one, Amelia had an English accent, short mousy hair and wore very mannish clothing. I had heard Mummy and Richard whispering together that perhaps they were of the Sapphic inclination. Neither of them wanted to go shooting, but they had declared that boating and horse-riding were acceptable, and they professed to adore Scottish castles.

We also had a family group staying, a London married couple who went shooting but were not particularly good shots. They thought they might like to ride as well and dilly-dallied trying to make up their minds and finally decided not. They were in their mid-thirties and had rather posh accents and terribly smart clothes. Their son was perhaps eight years old and rather strange. Most days he would go with his nanny down to the loch. He would sit on the edge of the water staring moodily into the smooth, glassy surface and throw pebbles with short, sharp aggressive movements, like a marionette with someone unpractised pulling the strings. Perhaps if I had been more noble, I would have suggested that he come out riding with us. I knew that Linda had several very reliable little ponies, but there was something peevish and unattractive about this boy. He had a weak receding chin and eyes liked boiled gooseberries, and I just couldn't bring myself to have anything to do with him. He rather reminded me of some of the more unpleasant of the whimsical children in Mummy's books and that put me off.

Gwyneth and Amelia were driving the two miles to Linda's riding school in their rather smart saloon car, a shiny British racing-green. I had told John, one of the stable staff, of my plan to ride and he had obligingly given Balius a very thorough grooming, and had even washed out his thick silvery tail, which he had then finger-combed carefully, so that it was as full and luxuriant as any owner of a show pony could desire.

We rode down the road, and I enjoyed some moments of solitude; making conversation with guests and staff members all day could get rather tiring, even for such a chatterbox as myself. Let me just describe Balius to those of you who may not have read any of my previous books. He was, of course, beautiful – a grey gelding, mainly thoroughbred but with some Highland pony blood in him. He was only young, but already we had begun competing, and he was going very well. I had high hopes of him. I also have a lovely, sweet part-Arab chestnut mare, called Copperplate. She is an experienced jumper, and I had bought her as a schoolmaster, or in her case a schoolmistress – but that doesn't sound quite right?

Just few weeks previously, I had discovered that a stallion that Mark was training had escaped and jumped into Copperplate's field. Now, there was a chance that she was in foal. I hadn't told anyone. I had been unsure of the legality of the situation. If she were in foal, would the owners expect me to pay a stud fee? I decided to say nothing. The stallion was the most fabulous golden animal, a strange pearlescent colour. He looked like a magnificent steed of the gods. Mark was supposed to be teaching him to jump.

Mark Lansdowne was, to say the very least, a rather tiresome individual, my stepfather's nephew. He made no bones about the fact that he disliked my mother and me and considered us money-hungry interlopers. The other morning, I had been lurking in the background, watching him ride the golden stallion, and he had been employing his usual strong-arm, stand-over-merchant tactics. The stallion had reacted aggressively, all macho and determined that he was the boss. They had gone over a few of the jumps, and the stallion certainly had oodles of athleticism and power. I hoped that if Copperplate was in foal, then the offspring would inherit her quiet equitable nature and the stallion's glorious colour and physique.

The other issue in this complicated secret was that in the near future, I would not be able to compete on Copperplate. That would take me back down to just one horse. I know this sounds incredibly spoilt and greedy, but for so many years now, I had always had two mounts. In my youth, there had been my loyal first pony, Black Boy, and then Rapide, a very cheeky bay show jumper. Whenever I think about my two original ponies, I sigh wistfully, remembering regretfully, how I had been persuaded to sell them. In the still watches of the night, I often wake and wonder what had become of them. I had lost touch with the family who had bought both of them and feared that they might have been separated and adrift in the world, at the mercy of people who were not horsey.

Gwyneth and Amelia arrived at the riding school before I got there. I could hear them assuring Linda that they were both competent riders and she directed them over to two of her sturdy cobs that were well-suited for taking riders of all types over the hills and along the sometimes rocky, narrow twisting tracks up on the moor.

We set off. There were eight of us in the party. Gwyneth and Amelia certainly hadn't lied: they were extremely capable riders. It was unusual to find such good riders hiring out horses but who was I to judge. If I were to go away for a holiday and there was riding available, of course, I would also want to see a new landscape from horseback, which is surely the best way to enjoy the scenic beauty.

Linda introduced me to two young helpers that had come to stay with her for a month. They were paying for their board but also helping out in exchange for free riding; they were tough kids called Scott and Mick from Birmingham with strong Brummy accents. I couldn't say that they were part of the 'great unwashed' as they positively reeked of carbolic soap as if their mothers had disinfected them before sending them up to Scotland. They could ride, after a fashion. They claimed to have learnt at a city farm in central Birmingham.

There were also two local girls who I had seen around in the village, Kirsty and Ellie. Kirsty had very curly black hair that boinged around as she moved, sticking out at all angles and when she donned her riding cap it looked rather odd as if she had stuck her hand in an electric socket. They were regulars at Linda's. The two of them rode on either side of me and pumped me for information about the goings-on at Blainstock and the upcoming filming of Macbeth which was to take place in the castle in the autumn. They asked if there was to be any work for local extras. I replied that I didn't know, but I would certainly enquire for them.

As we were all capable riders, we set off at a good speed, trotting and cantering along the narrow paths that wound between the gorse bushes and rocks. We planned to go around the loch and up into the hills beyond until we came to a stone ruin that had once been a very small castle that had guarded a valley. From there, it was even possible, on a clear day, to see the sea.

I was intrigued as I had never been this way before. I absolutely adore old ruins. They're so 'story book' and must appeal to the child in all of us. I imagined the doughty old Scots who might have lived there hundreds of years ago, without electricity, guarding their kingdoms against marauders, sitting around massive, log fires and chewing on meaty bones.

As we rode up the final hill, I gazed at the broken edifice. It was all that it had been promised; towering against the bright blue sky and looking down over a miniature valley that had once been somebody's kingdom. There was unusual emerald-green grass growing here and there, amidst the usual tumble of purple heather, golden gorse and weather-worn, grey rocks. The ruin had three good walls and even a part of a roof where one might have sheltered from the weather, but the rest was all broken-down scattered stones.

"See tha', green grass, that's where they would 'ave buried tha dead bodies of tha enemies," declared Mick.

"Mebbe we could dig up sum bones," suggested Scott.

"You boys have a taste for the gruesome, don't you," said Linda laughing.

We all dismounted and Linda produced some chocolate bars out of her saddlebag. The horses cropped the sweet summer grass that was growing around the old stones.

"You can see this must have had about four rooms," said Linda. "Those three walls would have been the main hall and then there would have been a collection of smaller rooms."

The boys rushed over to explore, clambering over the rocks and shouting to each other, pretending to be kings of the castle and calling each other a dirty rascal.

"Watch out boys, it could be dangerous," shouted Linda.

"Do ya think this ol' castle 'as got ghosts?" asked one of the boys.

"I's jus' like out of 'em Famous Five books," said the other.

"Can you reach this place by car?" asked Gwyneth.

"There is an old track, but it's rarely used, it comes off the road from the tiny hamlet, Rossiter," explained Linda.

"There must be hundreds of these old ruins, scattered across the Highlands," said Amelia.

"Probably," said Linda. "This is the only one within an hour or so of riding distance from us."

"I would love to ride to the sea," said Gwyneth, standing and shielding her eyes against the sun which blazed down on us.

"Yes, we can do a whole day's ride, if you like," said Linda. "Should I arrange it?"

"Oh, yes, please," said Gwyneth.

"Jill, do you think you can get away from the castle for a whole day?" asked Linda.

"I'll have to ask Mummy," I replied regretfully.

"We wanna go ta the sea," chorused the urchins from Birmingham.

"You shall go to the sea," said Linda with a fond smile.

We mounted and went back the way we had come. Balius trod carefully around the steep track that wound around the hills. I could see from the sun that it was almost midday and I wondered what Cook had packed for my lunch. As usual, I was starving.

Gwyneth and Amelia thanked Linda and paid her in crisp new pound notes and drove back to the castle in time for the buffet lunch that would be set out in the dining room for those guests not out shooting. I sat down in the tack room with Linda and sharing my delicious ham and mustard sandwiches with her and the two boys. Then, we cleaned the tack that we had used this morning.

"Have you got any more riders today?" I asked.

"Yes, I've got some of my regulars from the village coming up for a lesson. Those two women, they've booked a ride to the sea on Friday. I hope you can come Jill. It should be fun."

"I'm sure Mummy will agree. I'll get Cook to make up a hamper for all of us. If Bonnie can be spared, I'll bring her as a packhorse. It will make it more like a proper trek. Do you think you might rope in a few of your regulars, and we can have a jolly jamboree?" I asked enthusiastically.

"I'll ring around," said Linda. "The weather forecast is good."

On Thursday I cleaned rooms and dusted like a demon. Then I went down and helped cook cutting up onions, carrots and turnips, to add to the venison stew that was one of her specialities. The guests liked everything to be very Scottish.

"The trick is a shake of cinnamon," she told me confidingly.

The following morning, I woke with that wonderful feeling of anticipation – a whole day's riding – my idea of utter bliss!

"Where are you off to today?" asked Mark, making a surprise appearance in the stables when I was getting ready to leave.

"We're riding to the sea," I replied evenly. I hated talking to Mark but tried not to antagonise him. I was afraid one day there was going to be a blazing row, from which there would be no return to even a semblance of politeness.

"What are *you* doing today?" I asked.

"Nothing to do with you!" he retorted and turned on his heel.

"He be ridin' that gold stallion," said John, to me quietly when there was no risk of being overheard.

"He's a nice horse," I said casually, and John grunted assent.

I rode out of the yard. Balius nodded his head a few times at me as if to say, 'be careful'. He would know, of course, that Copperplate and the stallion had been in together, that she might be in foal. He was very conspiratorial, was my Balius. Bonnie, who was actually Balius's mother, walked beside us with the packsaddle. The food was stashed in big bags securely strapped. There were a range of delicious sandwiches, shortbread, and apples. Linda was supplying drinks.

There were a whole bunch of us this time. The two young women guests, Gwyneth and Amelia, the Brummy boys, Scott and Mick. I had been attempting to improve my name-remembering techniques, and I noticed that Scott had a few fat freckles on his squashy nose, and Mick was shorter and rounder with a funny shaped left ear. And there were six children from the village; Kirsty and Ellie again, and also their cousins who lived in a big house down near the kirk. I can't even begin to try to remember their names.

The sky was overcast, but Linda looked up and pronounced that it should clear by mid-morning. We rode up by the loch. Mr Arthur Branson, the accountant who might have been the Laird of Blainstock Castle but for the gambling folly of his ancestor, was sitting on a rock on the other side of the water. I waved cheerily, but he turned away as if he hadn't seen me. The water rippled deep blue and grey this morning.

"You know tha Loch Nessie monster, it ever bin seen here?" asked the freckled Scott.

"Not to my knowledge," said Linda, not bothering to tell him that that was an entirely different loch.

"Coo! That would be somefin, wouldn't it, to tell 'em back home," said Mick, "we seen the monster an'all."

"You need to keep your eyes peeled," said Gwyneth in clear ringing tones, her Scottish accent bouncing around the hills.

"What 'appens when ya boil a funny bone?" asked Scott, who seemed rather keen on riddles.

"I don't know," said Linda.

"You get a laughing stock!" he quipped.

"That's very good!" I declared.

The horses walked steadily, winding around the little path, nose to tail. Linda was riding a frisky little skewbald mare, her long legs stretched down almost to the backs of the pony's knees.

"That mare is new, isn't it?" I asked.

"Yes, I'm training her for the summer, taking her out and about. She's only just been backed, and her owners have gone to the south of France. They want her to be ready for serious training in the autumn, and then junior show jumping next summer," she replied.

"She's very pretty, what is her name?"

"Puzzle."

I grimaced. "Not exactly original."

"I know," said Linda, "but it does suit her. She's got a few twists and turns in her behaviour."

It was nearly three hours riding before we reached the top of the hill that overlooked the blue-lapped coastline that wound its way in curls and long sweeps along the edge of the sea. The beach was not fine white sand as one might find on the south of France, but rather crunched up rosy shells that shone with a pearly lustre in the sunlight that was breaking through the streaked clouds.

"Tha tis! Tha tis!" shouted Mick.

"I saw it first!" argued Scott.

The two of them pushed their horses at a rough trot down the hill.

"Hold hard, you boys!" shouted Linda. "Or the ponies will fall and break their knees."

"Sorry Miss," said Scott.

"As soon as we get to the beach, we'll hold the horses, and you can run in and splash around," said Linda.

"It'll be icy cold," said Amelia.

"Bracing, I think is the word," said Gwyneth.

We spent two hours lounging on the beach, taking it in turns to hold the reins of the horses. The Brummy boys splashed and shrieked and were running in and out of the water, their skinny white bodies purple with cold. The children from the village joined them, and Linda, Gwyneth, Amelia and I gossiped about the latest films, fashions and books. We all ate sandwiches, shortbread and apples before we set off for home.

"There's a good gallop across the sand here," said Linda.

The air was pure crystal, and I took deep breaths, thinking how good this oxygen must be for my brainpower. Perhaps Mummy should come down and breathe the air to help make her unborn baby more intelligent.

We were soon galloping across the crunchy surface. The horses loved it. I pushed Balius into the shallowest of the water, and the icy spray was flung up by his drumming hoofs and hit my face. I could taste the briny flavour in my mouth.

"I'm tha fastest!" called out Scott as he and Mick raced neck and neck at the front of the crowd. Gwyneth and Amelia stayed back so the boys could feel as if they were winning, their sturdy brown trekking ponies making a valiant effort to pretend to be racehorses.

"It was a tie, neck and neck," said Linda.

"You weren't near enuff ta see," scoffed Scott. "I was tha first."

"No, you weren't," whined Mick.

By the time we got back to the riding school we had that lovely tired feeling that one gets after a long but enjoyable ride. Linda directed Scott and Mick, and with the insatiable energy of the young they unsaddled and pushed ponies into loose boxes, filled up hay nets and buckets of water. The six girls from the village were also mucking in before being picked up by one of their relatives in a van.

"I see you've got plenty of help. I'll ride back to the castle," I said.

Balius was still bouncing along on the way home, and I was happy to see that he was fit. He was beginning to mature and would soon be at his peak.

"Jill, I've run a bath for you. We've got a special dinner on tonight. Make sure you dress up," said Mummy.

"Why, what is it?" I asked.

"We've got a trio of fiddlers coming, and after dinner we're going to have an impromptu dance. Push back the dining room table and make up some sets."

"My goodness!" I exclaimed, "I'm not sure that my Scottish dancing will be up to much!"

"Don't worry, apparently Gwyneth is an expert, and she is going to teach us," said Mummy.

"Is Mr Branson going to join in?" I asked a little mischievously.

"I don't know. I hope that he will enjoy it, harking back to his ancestors."

"What do you think it must be like for him, knowing that this castle could have belonged to his family, if only his great-great-uncle hadn't lost it?" I asked.

"I have no idea, but he seems to bear no malice. Merely a gentle interest," said Mummy, distractedly. "I have to go and talk to Cook. Hurry up and get ready. I'd like you to serve drinks with me outside in the courtyard."

The evening was an absolute riot. The grouse-shooters had had a good day and brought back bags of plump, dead birds, which to them was a splendid success, but to me was rather gruesome. They all drank copious amounts of red wine and boasted and bragged and attempted to talk in Scottish accents. Two of them were older women, at least sixty years old, very stout and formidable, wearing hats from which pheasant feathers sprouted. They were sisters who claimed to have been shooting grouse since they were three years old. I imagined that they had been blasting away at anything rustling in a hedgerow ever since. They both were very similar in appearance with the look of later-life Queen Victoria, speaking with booming voices. They insisted on partnering each other.

There was a group of four young men who brayed with upper-class accents and worked in the same bank in the city. They claimed that this was a 'work-do' where they were able to get to know each other in an alternative environment, team building which was apparently the latest thing. They each drove a flashy car and had insisted on individual rooms, which was certainly good for business for the castle. Team-building obviously had its limits. The parents of the odd little boy, but not the nanny, were there. The mother was dressed in the most exquisitely well-cut full-length pale-pink silk gown with a few subtle ruffles and swirls in just the right places. She looked utterly divine, ethereal like a celestial being who had floated in by moonlight.

Mummy was looking rather tired and excused herself after the meal. She was obviously finding the burden of running the castle full of guests to be rather taxing in her delicate state. The baby was due in about seven months. Apparently, the first trimester is one of the hardest, in terms of feeling tired and sick.

The fiddlers were amazing. They looked like three chubby little hobbits dressed in green and red. I half-expected their tapping feet to be all hairy. They jigged and juggled their fiddles, in time with the music and then Hugh, who played the bagpipes every morning as a wake-up call for the guests, came and joined in. John made up the numbers for the sets, and he knew how to dance. His feet were flying nimbly in the steps and I was amazed. I felt like a big clodhopper in comparison, but I was certainly in demand with the four bankers, and they swung me this way and that enthusiastically. It was rather fun!

We danced relentlessly for hours and past midnight, the last of us were sitting around together. We'd waved off the fiddlers and John and Hugh were moving the dining room table back to its customary position when a shout from outside sent us to the window.

Part II

There were horses flying around the courtyard, dark shapes like creatures from the heavens that had swooped down onto earth. We ran outside in a bunch, exclaiming and stumbling in our evening dress.

"The gate, the gate!" called Hugh and he was running like a deer in his tartan trews and little button-up shoes, but he was too late. Several of Mark's horses galloped wildly before him and through the courtyard entrance. We could hear their hoofs thudding in the cool night air, their iron shoes striking sparks on the stones. I heaved a sigh of relief when I saw that Balius was still in the courtyard, he hadn't got through to gallop across the moorland. I hated to think what might happen to those big thoroughbreds, unused to trekking across the moors, slipping and stumbling over the rough, stony, twisting tracks.

"Come on Jill. We must be away after them. I'll see if they've all gone. How did they get out?" asked John in anguish, as if he thought he might be to blame. But that was unlikely. One might perhaps not latch the odd stable door correctly, but every one of them. That was beyond the bounds of probability.

"Someone must have let them out," said Richard, a worried frown on his face.

"All Mark's horses and the golden stallion!" I cried. "Someone is going to have to ring up Mark and let him know. Not me!"

"I'll do that. Hugh, John, Jill you go out and see if there are any left in the stable yard. You can fetch Bonnie up from the field. Perhaps Linda can help us. She knows the country well," said Richard.

It didn't take long to get organised. Every single stable door had been opened and was swinging ajar. This was an act of utter and deliberate treachery.

"We've got Bonnie and Copperplate. They were both out in the field," said Hugh. "Miss Jill you take the saddle and bridle back to the castle and get Balius ready. John, you get Bonnie and Copperplate down. I'll gather together some stuff. We need to take some oats and headcollars to see if we can find them and fetch them back."

"The moon's full," said John.

"Aye," said Hugh. "It's as bright as day out there. Go, get to it!"

I ran back to the courtyard, and Balius stood for me. He was hanging his head a little as if embarrassed that he had joined in the general naughtiness.

Within thirty minutes Hugh, John and I had set out. We took torches, and Hugh riding Copperplate was following the tracks. The ground was hard and dry, and there wasn't much to see, but there were piles of dung here and there, and we thought it likely they would have headed for the loch, which was the regular track that was followed by walkers and riders leaving the castle.

The vanilla moon was high in the sky, and I wondered at the beauty of the night. I decided that in future a few rides by moonlight might be rather fun.

"Mr Micheldever will have rung Linda McNally, and she'll ride up the road, checking that none of them have strayed that way. I imagine they'll stick together," said Hugh. His face was grim, his mouth a straight line of unhappiness. As stable manager, he would have to take responsibility.

Balius threw his head up and whinnied, looking over to the left of the track.

"Stop, shhh," said Hugh.

"I can hear something beyond that hill," said John. "That's where the wee spring is and the sweet green grass."

We turned the horses and climbed up a small round hill. From the top, we could see down into a dip in the ground and there were at least some of the horses there.

"That big stallion will be the ringleader," said Hugh. "We need to go carefully. We don't want them running off again. Miss Jill, you dismount and take the reins of these three and John, and I will go down with the oats and halters."

I stood on the hill, and Balius was nervous, sniffing the air and pawing with his front hoof. Bonnie and Copperplate were more docile and put their heads down to crop at the thin summer grass.

The opposite hill threw a black shadow over the horses, and I couldn't see how many there were. I did recognise the big golden stallion who threw his head up, like a wild mustang, now he had seen us. I wondered if he might come charging up the hill when he smelled the two mares. I hoped not. I hadn't had any experience of stallions, and I had always been told that they weren't suitable for children.

"Co-op, co-op," said Hugh's deep voice. I saw him walk quietly up to the big golden horse with his hand out, probably tempting him with oats. The stallion allowed him to approach and then dipped his head and Hugh slipped on the halter.

"You catch the big gelding over there, the grey one, Mr Mark's favourite," said Hugh to John. The horses were quiet now. I could see that they weren't wild mustangs. They were essentially domesticated creatures that had got loose and run away, but now they were happy to return to their comfortable stables. John slipped the halter on the big grey horse that I knew was Mark's favourite for Badminton next year. Then John caught the brown gelding, called Mustard, who was the big grey horse's friend. He led them both back towards Hugh and me, followed by the stallion.

"You lead the brown from Balius, Miss Jill, and John will lead the grey and Copperplate from Bonnie, and I'll bring the stallion up behind us. The others should follow. I'm not sure that they're all here but at least most of them."

We got back to the stables, a solemn line of horses, with the rest following of their own accord. Horses are like sheep. They like to hang out together. Rarely is there one that careers off on their own. This was what made it so strange. Hugh did a headcount.

"That Jewel is missing," said he worriedly.

Jewel was a beautiful mare which Mark had brought to the stables a few months ago. At the time, I had noticed her because she was a strange creamy colour. I remember thinking that she shone like a soft, lustrous pearl. I had wondered at the time that she was only 15.2 hh, much smaller than any of Mark's other horses.

Mark had just arrived at the stables, and far from looking relieved and grateful that we had recaptured nearly all the horses, he was stomping around in a rage.

"You fool," he shouted at Hugh. "You must have left all the doors open, what sort of moron are you?"

Richard had now arrived on the scene and looked at Mark with a shocked expression.

"Mark – a word!" he barked, in a voice, that I had never heard before. In the past, Richard had always been the most easy-going and kindest of people. Somehow, I found it reassuring to discover that he had a backbone of steel and would stand up to the bullies in this world!

"What are we going to do?" I asked John. "Should we go back out and see if we can find the mare?"

"I doan know," said John. "It is strange that she wasn't with the others."

In the end, Richard decreed that we all go to bed and we would search for the mare in the morning. With any luck, she would come back of her own accord, and we would find her in the stable yard, or up by the gate with Bonnie and Copperplate. We trooped off to bed, and I slept lightly. I found myself listening in the quiet night air for the sound of hoofs and then when I finally slept, I dreamt that Balius and Copperplate had run away together, to make a better life for themselves.

I went down to breakfast, and Mummy was up and fussing over the buffet, making sure that each of the delicious dishes was ready for the guests.

"Jill, I absolutely insist that you eat something before you go rushing all over the countryside looking for that mare," she said, with a worried line between her eyes.

"What does Richard think?" I asked. "Did someone deliberately let those horses out? Do you think it might be one of the guests," I continued my ruminations in a stage whisper.

I helped myself to a plateful of scrambled eggs with three large crispy bacon rashers.

"Or perhaps it is one of Mark's competitors, someone with a grudge against him," I said, my face lighting up at this rather interesting scenario.

"Shhh, shhh," said Mummy as Arthur Branson came down for his breakfast. As usual, slipping into his seat quietly and unobtrusively.

I looked down into my plate at fluffy, golden eggs but my thoughts were scrambling. Arthur's family had lost the castle in a card game. Perhaps he had come to avenge their honour - to cause trouble. He had slipped away while we were dancing and opened all the stable doors. I looked at him sideways. He was carefully buttering a piece of toast, looking innocent and unassuming. It's always the quiet ones, I thought darkly.

I wondered what a proper detective would do at this point, in order to discover the culprit. The obvious thing would be to search the rooms of the guests to discover some clues to their dark and dastardly motives.

"I've been over to see Hugh, and there's no sign of that Jewel," said Richard, striding in from the door that came from the kitchen.

"Oh dear! Oh dear!" lamented Mummy. She hated it when things went wrong. She liked everything to be happy and pleasant, like the worlds she described in her children's books.

"Jill I'll sort out the guests' bedrooms, you must go and help look for Jewel."

"No, no," I replied earnestly. "I insist on helping with the rooms first. There'll be plenty of people to help with the search."

Now, you're probably wondering, dear readers, why I should prefer to clean bedrooms rather than riding across the moorland looking for a lost horse. Or perhaps you have guessed? Jill the Super Sleuth. I wanted to search the rooms, just like a real Lady Detective and see if I could find some clues to this dreadful crime. In particular, I wanted to search Arthur Branson's room as I felt that there might be the key to the mystery. Mummy gave me an odd 'motherly' look. Sometimes, I suspected that she could read my mind, even though she often declared that what went on in my head was a mystery to her.

I gathered together my housemaidly accessories and innocently made my way up the stairs and along to the west wing where the guests' bedrooms lay. I walked to the end of the corridor and entered Arthur Branson's room. It was only a single, and I saw that, as usual, he had made his own bed. This was the personality that he constantly presented, unassuming, modest and not wanting to be a bother to anyone. It would be perfect cover, for someone bent on revenge for a historical wrongdoing. He had a book beside his bed which he must have got from the castle library, a history of the local area. Perhaps he was looking for clues about his lost inheritance. I dusted the carved wooden bedhead and the surface of the bedside table, then casually flicked through the pages of the book in case he had left any incriminating notes to himself. Then I moved to the wardrobe. There were no clothes left lying around, but still I opened it. There were a few shirts neatly hanging and a city suit that no doubt he intended to wear on his return to Edinburgh. His suitcase sat neatly at the bottom of the wardrobe and looking around, hastily I clicked it open; some spare clothes, toiletries, and a travelling clock in a green leather fold-up case. Then I spied it, a bundle of documents with faded copper plate writing across the front of browned, stiff envelopes, tied together with an old pink ribbon. Here was the clue!

My heart was beating very quickly, and I felt my fingers fumbling nervously. Then I heard a screech. Not loud, but distinctive. I froze, thinking that Mr Branson was about to burst in and find me sneaking through his personal belongings. There was a silence then I could hear the rattle of whispering voices, arguing, coming from the next room.

That was Gwyneth and Amelia.

"It will … too odd … " said one of them.

"I don't …." said the other.

I couldn't tell which was which and I couldn't make out the other words.

This decided me. I couldn't risk reading Arthur's private correspondence. It would be too mortifying to be caught out in the act. Quickly I shut the wardrobe doors and began to sweep the floor. Never was I more thankful for my change of mind as in the next minute the door opened and Mr Branson came in.

"I'm terribly sorry to disturb you," he said as if he had come into my room, not his own.

"Not at all, just general housekeeping," I said, feeling that I had to make an excuse for being there.

"I thought I might get my jacket and hike up the hills and see if I can't spot that horse that has gone missing," he said very politely.

"What a good idea!" I responded in a robust and mock-jolly voice.

Then I packed up my kit and slipped out. Usually, the next room would be Gwyneth and Amelia, but we tried to avoid the rooms of guests when they were within.

I finished half of the cleaning, and it was time for my mid-morning break. I went and sat down in the kitchen and watched Cook at her work. She plonked a big bowl of peas in front of me to be shelled, and I set to work. I was deep in thought. How did one begin to operate as a Super Sleuth? I decided that I would have to be methodical and make a series of lists. There should be a list of possible motives and another for those with the opportunity to commit the crime. I wouldn't be able to call the guests in for questioning as I was 'unofficial', but I might try and remember, and ask Mummy and Richard if they could recall who had been in the room when the horses came galloping into the courtyard. But Mummy had retired? That meant she had opportunity. This thought threw me a little – but surely she could be ruled out? I realised then that this was going to be much more complicated than I had first thought. It might not have been an 'inside' job. Perhaps an outsider had snuck in and let the horses out. Malevolent Mark would undoubtedly have made some enemies in his ruthless rise up the eventing ladder.

I had to make a list of guests and see who could remember who was in the room at the time. As far as outsiders went, I would have to ask in the village if there had been any strangers around. I began to get quite excited about this detecting lark, determined that I would track down the bounders who had wreaked such havoc with the precious horses. The worst thing was that Jewel was still missing.

I tried to remember exactly where I had been just before the horses had galloped into the courtyard. Most of the guests had left the room, and there were just a few of us sitting around at the end of the evening.

Richard had definitely been there, and Hugh and John. I wracked my brain, who else had still been in the room? I remembered that one of the braying young men had been drinking up the last of a bottle of red wine, and one of the two old sisters and I thought perhaps Gwyneth. It was extraordinarily difficult to think back accurately. It had been a long and jolly evening, and I had been exhausted riding all day to the sea and then dancing all night. I would have to ask Richard. Perhaps his recall was more accurate than mine.

"Jill dear, the girls from the village can finish the work," said Mummy, coming in and looking very tired. She hated unpleasantness, and what had happened last night had been extraordinarily unpleasant. Poor Mummy, she didn't deserve this.

"I can go out after lunch," I said. "I'll just go back and help the girls. I really must Do My Bit, especially in these Times of Trouble."

"If you like," said Mummy and flapped her hands ineffectually and wafted away.

I trudged upstairs and thought I might do the room of the two older women, the ones of a certain age. Only one of them had been in the room when the horses galloped by, the other had supposedly gone upstairs. Although I couldn't think of any obvious motive. Perhaps they had a beloved niece who was a three-day eventer, and Mark had somehow crossed her, if not in love, then in a competition. I would make sure there were no photographs on their bedsides of young people riding three-day eventing horses.

I entered their room and began making the beds, dusting the bedside cabinets and sweeping the floor. There were no family photos on display. I risked a quick look in their wardrobe and saw nothing suspicious. Although I knew they were in the shooting party, I didn't want to risk them discovering me snooping. I imagined that such feisty individuals would be capable of both apoplexy and icy fury in equal measure. I shuddered at the thought. I swept the same patch of floor repeatedly as it suddenly occurred to me that they might be stalwart and loyal supporters of another grouse-shooting business and perhaps they wanted to drive Richard out of business.

I shut their door behind me. I had about a hundred questions to ask Richard. Perhaps he had some ideas about what had happened. I needed to speak to him, but he was up on the moors with the shooters and wouldn't be back until the evening.

I went down to the stables to ask if Jewel had returned. Both Hugh and John were out searching for her and they had left one small stable boy in charge. Linda rode into the yard on Puzzle, the sweet but naughty little skewbald mare.

"Yups!" I called out to her.

"Hullo Jill. What a drama last night! I rode off down the road and back again, but it seems they had gone up on the moor. How is Mark taking it?"

That was a good question. So far, he had blamed Hugh, but I didn't believe that would be the end of it. Sooner or later, he was sure to create a positive avalanche of wrath at this episode.

"I don't know. None of the horses have come to any harm, but Jewel is still missing," I replied.

"Do you want to ride out with me?" asked Linda.

"Where should we go?" I asked.

"Hugh has left instructions about the direction in which he and John were going," said Linda, "we have to look in the office."

She dismounted, or rather stepped off the small mare and strode on her long legs over to the office. I brought Balius out of the stable and began to tack up. He was looking eager and interested as if he knew something was afoot.

We headed to the track around the shore of the loch and then planned to strike out in another direction to that which had been taken by Hugh and John.

"How is your business going?" I asked. I was always concerned that Linda was eking out a very small living with her riding school. Her main sources of income seemed to be training other people's horses; and buying and selling horses that she had re-trained herself.

"It's not bad, I'm making decent money training Puzzle, and there's a few more been promised me. The local riders are ticking over, and, of course, riders from the castle are always welcome," she replied.

I watched her riding Puzzle. The mare had been jig-jogging the other day, but today she was walking out with long, balanced strides. I found myself constantly admiring Linda's horsemanship.

"So, what do you think happened that night?" I asked. "With the horses being let out."

She looked into the distance in a thoughtful manner.

"You've got an idea, haven't you?" I asked.

"Not really. I guess it depends on the motive. Was there a motive? Or was it just mischief-making? Someone with bats in the belfry?"

"I hadn't even thought of that," I replied. "I was considering whether or not it was an inside job, one of the guests, or someone from outside. Someone with a grudge against Mark."

"Perhaps it was you," she said mischievously. "You're not very fond of your step-cousin."

"That's an understatement," I muttered darkly.

"Look at that strange little boy!" said Linda. He was crouching by the side of the loch while his nanny sat some distance away on a rug, reading a novel.

"He is rather odd," I said.

He had very white hair, and with his pale skin he looked like a smudge of light, a ghost.

"You know the first sign of a psychopath is torturing animals during childhood," said Linda.

"Do you think he is torturing animals?" I asked.

There was a moment's silence between us. Birds overhead called, and the light reflecting off the loch sparkled in a long beam, as if pointing towards the hills.

"Or do you think he did it? As a form of extreme mischief?" I asked.

"I'm not accusing anyone," said Linda. "I think we should keep looking at the ground, trying to find hoofprints."

We both dropped out eyes to the ground and searched for marks.

"As far as I can see, they didn't come this way, but the ground is so hard you'd need to be a Native American tracker to distinguish just the faint outline of a print. The ones, the horses that we found, they headed off over to the hills in the west. Almost as if they were thinking of going to the seaside, but by a more circuitous route than the one we normally ride across."

"Do you think they fancied a seaside jaunt; charabancs, ice-creams and sandcastles?" asked Linda, a glint in her eye.

"Well, I wouldn't blame Mark's horses for wanting to get away from him for a while," I retorted.

"That golden stallion, he's a strange animal," said Linda. "He looks vaguely American, you know like a palomino but his mane and tail are the same golden colour as his hide."

"Yes, he's certainly a fine-looking animal. But he has a rather uncertain temperament," I said dismissively. I had a huge admiration for Linda, but I didn't want to tell her that the stallion had mated with Copperplate. It might put her in an invidious position. Nor did I want to show any untoward interest in the animal. Although, I was insanely curious to know who might own him and what was his breeding.

We trotted on towards the path that we would have followed if we had gone to the sea, but we didn't see Jewel.

"Are those women, Gwyneth and Amelia wanting to do any more riding?" asked Linda.

"I don't know, they've only got three days to go. They set off in their fancy-schmanzy car today with a picnic hamper."

We rode on still searching fruitlessly for hoofprints and then turned disconsolately for home.

"I've got to get back, I'm doing all the work myself now," said Linda. "The two boys were picked up by their uncle yesterday. Apparently, one of their kin is ill."

"That's a shame," I said. "They seemed to love it up here. Hopefully, they can come back next holidays."

Part III

I got back to the castle, and it was time for dinner. We all assembled in the courtyard, and I decided that this was a good time to do my Miss Marple thing and watch and listen to the way that people were interacting. I wasn't sure exactly what I was watching for – perhaps aberrant behaviour – but then a practiced criminal was going to be a master of 'looking normal'. I wished now that I had read more detective novels, rather than my usual fare of pony books and tomes on equestrian information and techniques.

The conversation soon moved to the excitement of the night before. Richard looked uneasy. He wanted his guests to remember their stay in quite a different way, not a malicious event by an unknown perpetrator.

"Have all the horses been recovered?" asked one of the young men from the city.

"There's still one mare unaccounted for," admitted Richard. "But we've got people riding over the hills searching for her."

"I kept an eye out when I went down to the loch," said Mr Branson quietly. I looked at him from under my lashes. He seemed so harmless and unassuming, but outward appearances could be deceptive.

I particularly watched the smart couple with the gormless child who didn't eat with us in the dining room. They were looking uncomfortable. And they were silent. Then the father spoke up and tried to change the subject, for which Richard would be thankful.

"The shooting went well today. I believe there was more in my bag than on any previous day," he volunteered.

"By Jove, you're right there," said one of the young men. "I do believe my aim is getting better. Or perhaps the grouse are flying slower." He laughed heartily at what he must have imagined was an amusing remark, and his three companions joined in. Surely, they were too stupid to have conceived even such a simplistic plot as to open the stable doors.

Perhaps this first act of letting the horses go was just the prelude to a much more serious crime. A bit of a diversion. I believe they call that a red herring in the detective world. I decided that I would cast my net a little wider and go down to the village and ask if there had been any strangers in the area. And I wanted to keep an eye on that little boy. I had found out that his name was Percival – what a name!

The next morning, I was on full-time duty cleaning rooms as there was only one girl from the village coming up. Apparently, there was a local market in a nearby town, and it was a highlight of the summer. I made beds, dusted and swept as if my life depended on it, and then leaning on my broom handle I engaged the local girl in conversation.

"What are they saying in the village about the horses getting out?" I asked.

She looked rather disinterested.

"I'm not sure that it's such big news. You see on that same night there was an incident at the local pub, and Jimmy McCorker and Malcolm Hamilton were at each other and had to be pulled apart, and the local constable turned up. It was a bit of a shenanigan."

I had no idea who Jimmy McCorker and Malcolm Hamilton were, but, apparently, this excitement far eclipsed a few loose horses up at the castle. Still, I persisted in my questioning.

"Did you see any strange people, or cars in the village on that day? Strange – as in people you don't know."

She screwed up her face and then told me she had been at the castle all day, not down in the village. That made sense. I decided that I would drive down and ask at the local shop.

After I had finished my cleaning, I popped my head into the kitchen and asked Cook if she needed anything from the village.

"Well now Miss Jill, that's very thoughtful of you, I could do with a bottle of vanilla essence," she replied.

"Right-o, I'm onto it," I said and bolted for the Land Rover. I took the two deerhounds that had been feeling neglected since our guests' arrival. They might be getting lots of pats, and oohs and aahs but not decent, long, brisk walks. They were absolute giants, as big as Shetland ponies, and it had taken me a while to get used to them as Mummy and I had never had dogs at Chatton, just my ponies and Mummy's hens. They loped after me and jumped into the back of the Land Rover.

It didn't take long to whizz down the road to the village. It was the same as the general store in Chatton where Mrs Buzzby knew everything about everybody. I walked in, and it was like a very cramped and dusty Aladdin's Cave, with crowded narrow shelves groaning with every possible product and concoction. I couldn't find the vanilla essence, but the shop woman located it for me.

"I was just wondering, were there any strange vehicles, or people in or out of the village last Friday?" I asked innocently.

"Arrh.." she replied knowingly. "I've already told the constable, there was a Land Rover with a horse trailer came through, didn't stop, just drove on straight through. I had never seen it before."

"Gosh!" I said, my mouth agape. "That's interesting!"

"Aye," she said knowingly, nodding vigorously as if she had just made a very important point in a vital argument.

I hot-footed it back to the castle.

"Mummy, did you know that there was an unknown Land Rover and horse trailer go through the village last Friday? It's been reported to the police."

"Yes, Richard did mention it. Listen, Jill, I really think you should stop worrying about this. Hugh is padlocking all the stable doors every night, and he's been taking it in turns with John to sleep in the yard. We think that it might just be a one-off."

"We think…" I said, suddenly feeling decidedly out of the loop. "You didn't say anything to me?" I replied plaintively, like a neglected child.

"I'm sorry darling. We didn't want to worry you," replied Mummy vaguely.

I walked away, muttering darkly about shutting stable doors after horses had bolted. The plot was thickening and in quite a different direction. It appeared that perhaps a particular horse had been targeted. Perhaps, Jewel was the answer. No-one had ever mentioned her before. I'd never seen anyone riding her. During the day she was out in a large yard or a small fenced field and brought in at night.

I strode down to the stables to find John sitting out in the yard, looking like he was a security guard.

"You've locked the stable doors after the horses have bolted!" I said in a jocular fashion, to try and begin this conversation on a light note. "Still no sign of Jewel?"

Hugh emerged from one of the loose boxes.

"Nay, she's been whisked away by the piskies," he said, and I remembered that he had a Cornish grandmother.

"Where exactly did Jewel come from, I've never seen anyone riding her?" I asked, my eyes wide in an innocent fashion.

Hugh squinted at me and chuckled.

"She arrived about three months ago. She goes out in the day and comes in at night. I got the feeling that Mark was thinking of breeding from her, but he never made that clear."

"The golden stallion!" I exclaimed.

"Now I didn't say that Miss Jill," said Hugh smiling at me.

"But that doesn't explain why somebody might be stealing her. I mean if you wanted to steal a horse wouldn't one of Mark's other horses be a more obvious target. Even if they had to export it to Europe so it wouldn't be recognised around here."

"That's a very fanciful mind you've got there!" said Hugh.

I had to go into dinner now. I walked back to the castle deep in thought. If letting the horses out of their stables had been a diversionary tactic, and it was Jewel who was the target then Mark would have the answers. Just as I was thinking about this he appeared, speeding in his snazzy little sportscar through the gate into the courtyard. It was the first time I'd seen him since we had brought the rest of the horses back from the moor on the fateful night.

"Joining us for dinner?" I asked him.

He bared his teeth at me in his usual nasty manner.

"That mare Jewel, she's still missing. What were you planning on doing with her?" I asked, deciding that direct questioning was one of the best ways of gaining information.

"None of your business," he snapped at me.

"Mark," said Richard appearing around the corner. "I would ask you to be civil to Jill and her mother when you are in *my* home."

There had been a distinct emphasis on the word 'my'. Hah! I thought. Mark is being cut out by this baby. He will no longer be the heir presumptive. No wonder he was increasingly sour.

"Are you joining us for dinner?" asked Richard. "Or have the police been in touch again?"

Mark paused. Obviously, he couldn't risk being rude to his uncle, who provided him with the stables, cross-country courses and training facilities. I had never really worked out how the finances with that situation stood. Although the stables were here at the castle, I wasn't sure who paid the bills. Nor was I really sure why Mark didn't have all this at Lansdowne House. That was a mystery that might be worth a little investigation I thought to myself. But first, if nothing else, I must satisfy my insatiable curiosity about Jewel.

"The police have not been in touch again. I just wanted to check that you haven't found Jewel. Thank you for the dinner invitation, but I'm pretty busy. I'm off to an event shortly with three horses. Thank you for improving the security, Richard." He added this last 'thanks' as a piece of token graciousness. But I did notice that the smile didn't quite reach his eyes.

I decided to leap in again, in for a penny, in for a pound.

"Can you tell us more about Jewel, Mark?" I asked.

He gave me a glowering look but did reply immediately. But, it would look too strange if he didn't.

"She was a six-year-old, 15.2 hh mare, cremello of indeterminate breeding." He reeled off these facts automatically, but his expression was murderous.

"Tell me, Mark, who did you *buy* her from?" said a ringing voice. I looked around, and there was Gwyneth, but she hadn't spoken with a Scottish accent, this time she sounded English.

He looked up at her and blanched. It was as if a thunderbolt had hit him.

"You!" he almost screeched.

"Yes Mark, me," she replied, giving him a sweet as sugar, but rather dangerous smile.

He looked white and shaky, like an anaemic blancmange. He turned on his heel and strode away.

As you can imagine I was utterly gobsmacked by this chain of events. Gwyneth wasn't Scottish, or at least she didn't sound Scottish. Amelia was by her side, and they walked away with quiet dignity and took a drink each from the tray. I looked at Richard and he looked at me. For once, I couldn't think of a thing to say. I leapt forward to go after them, to question them further, but Richard put his hand on my arm.

"I think Jill this is one you should leave well alone. Go and be the perfect hostess and *no questions*!"

You can imagine how I felt all through dinner. It was as if I would burst with imaginings. Unfortunately, Gwyneth was at the other end of the long table, and I couldn't even hear if she were speaking in a Scottish or an English accent. She had spoken to Mark in a challenging way, as if daring him to tell the truth. The emphasis on the word *buy* had been very noticeable. It dawned on me then that Gwyneth and Amelia had had something to do with the way in which the horses had been let loose and now the disappearance of Jewel.

After dinner, I usually slunk up to my room as I find polite conversation could get rather tedious. But tonight, I loitered. I could see Richard keeping an eye on me, and he had told me 'no questions', but I just couldn't resist.

"Gwyneth, I thought I heard you speaking in an English accent," I said. Please note this was technically a statement, not a question.

"Yes," she replied, now speaking English, "I'm afraid it was silly, but you see I rather pride myself on being able to speak in different accents, and Amelia had bet me that I couldn't keep up a Scottish accent throughout the course of our holiday. I guess I slipped up." She grinned at me. I smiled back. It was a perfect answer, but I didn't believe her for one moment.

"Jill," said Richard, swiftly manoeuvring himself to my elbow, "I wonder if you could go and help your mother in the kitchen. She and Cook are arranging the menus for tomorrow."

"Of course," I said and left the room. But I was determined that Gwyneth, Amelia and I were going to have a serious conversation. The Super Sleuth instinct in me told me that they knew more about the horses being let out of the stables and the disappearance of Jewel. It was simply a matter of time, and with Richard up on the moor every day there would be plenty of opportunities.

The next morning, I woke up thinking of the questions that I needed to ask. But the Super Sleuth instinct had let me down as I had forgotten that today was the day that Gwyneth and Amelia were leaving. I looked out the window of my bedroom and saw them piling their suitcases into the boot of their smart British racing-green saloon. I stood there utterly dismayed. They waved good-bye. For a moment, I thought that Gwyneth looked up at the window where I was standing and saluted me. Then the wheels of their car were spinning as they drove out the castle entrance gate. I had missed my chance!

The best I could do would be to casually look through Richard's papers and see if they had given an address when they had booked into the castle. But if I were planning a dastardly crime then I would have given a false address. Later that morning, with the semblance of being thoughtful and thorough, I went in and dusted the study. There in the list of bookings was Gwyneth's name and address and even I, the amateur, could see that it was unlikely to be correct.

Gwyneth Smith, 1 The Avenue, Highbrook, Oxfordshire (no phone number)

I could look up 'Highbrook' in the atlas, but I was sure that it didn't exist. "Smith" was certainly not original!

Well, I thought to myself, 'Game, Set and Match' to Miss Gwyneth Smith! I hadn't even written down the car registration plate. I decided that I was perhaps not cut out to be a Super Sleuth after all – perhaps not even a Minor Sleuth. I had read far too many pony books and not enough 'who dunnits'.

Later that day on my way down to Linda's, I found another clue, quite inadvertently. Actually, it was Balius who found it. He looked suspiciously and half-shied at a tangle of bright red by the roadside. I stopped and went back and looked down at the strange object. I dismounted and picked it up while Balius snorted a little gently, as if to tell me that this was important. It was a bright red wig. Gwyneth's wig! Now I knew for certain! It could be argued that the Scottish accent was merely a bet, but does one wear a bright red wig for the entire course of a holiday as part of a bet? And that remark she had made to Mark was etched in my memory,

"Tell me Mark, who did you *buy* her from?"

I began to analyse what she had said. 'tell me Mark', as if she knew him, and he had certainly recognised her. Then the emphasis on the word 'buy'.

I wondered if perhaps Mark had snatched the mare from her, not paid for her and then declared that he was keeping her. In my estimation of his character, this seemed entirely possible.

But if Gwyneth and Amelia were reclaiming a horse that they thought was rightfully theirs how could they have managed it? And I was almost certain that Gwyneth had been in the dining room when the horses had galloped into the courtyard. I couldn't remember exactly. This wouldn't rule out Amelia unbolting the stable doors. There was still the issue of how could Jewel have been spirited away. It was possible that Amelia had led her away and met someone with a horse trailer and they had loaded her and driven off into the night. It was possible, but full of risk. Amelia would have had to re-enter the castle and slip along to their room so she could appear innocently in the morning. What if she had been caught out and about when she had tried to come back?

My brain was brimming with these questions. I realised that not only committing a crime was pretty difficult. It seemed almost more difficult to work out who had committed it. I remembered how I had got involved in the dog smuggling and the excitement of delivering smuggled-in dogs all over the West country, but that had been planned by the others. I had been simply the driver. Essentially, I had done it for money, which thinking back was a sordid motive.

I arrived at Linda's for my riding lesson. I wanted to forge on with Balius's training. After a gruelling session with no stirrups on the lunge performing

all sorts of acrobatic exercises to 'strengthen my seat', Linda and I sat down for a cup of tea.

I told her all about my suspicions of Gwyneth and Amelia. She looked very thoughtful but remained silent.

"Linda, what do you think? I'm beside myself with this. I just can't work it out!" I pleaded with her.

"It does sound like she and Mark knew each other, and there was history between them concerning Jewel."

"Strangely, he didn't seem to want the police really involved. It was Richard who was talking to them."

"They would have needed accomplices," she said, shifting in her seat uncomfortably.

"Tell me what you're thinking!" I demanded.

"It's the boys, Scott and Mick, they disappeared that evening, picked up by their uncle after we got back from the ride. They took their stuff and disappeared up the road. I didn't actually see them leave in a vehicle. I've been waiting for someone to put two and two together and accuse them of the mischief. In fact, I've been dreading it. You see, I rather liked them."

I looked at her shocked. It was so obvious. I was amazed that no-one had accused the boys before. They were lower class, from Birmingham, you would have thought that they would have been prime suspects.

"So, you think they let the horses out. Perhaps their relative was the one in the Land Rover and the trailer. . . ." I said slowly.

"Perhaps they were Gwyneth and Amelia's accomplices. You know I always thought it was a bit strange, receiving this request from two random Brummy boys to come up here on a working holiday. I did ask them why they had contacted me, and not any other riding stable. They said that someone had told them how good it was here."

"You're right!" I exclaimed.

"I could have been flattered that my reputation had spread all the way down to the Midlands, but it did seem odd," she continued.

"How are we going to find out?" I asked, thinking of racing down to Birmingham.

"Why should we?" she asked coldly, and I could see a rather determined glint in her eye.

There was a long moment of silence stretching between us. I didn't know what to say. Suddenly I realised that in some ways I didn't know Linda at all.

"Don't you want to find out who did it?" I asked.

"I think I know, but it is none of my business. It was Jewel who was taken, and I think Mark hasn't pursued it because he knows that his actions might not look good. I liked Mick and Scott. I liked Gwyneth and Amelia."

"And I don't like Mark," I said.

This was a whole new scenario. I rode back to the castle, mired in thought. What had seemed like a jolly Enid Blyton mystery of goodies and baddies just wasn't that simple. Perhaps it was a case of none of my business. I argued back in my own head. Balius had been let out of his stable. But on the other hand, he had come to no harm.

In the very early hours of the morning, I woke with a start and sat up in the bed. The key to the mystery was the golden stallion. I would bet my last penny that Jewel was in foal to him. I lay down, and my thoughts were drifting as I went back to sleep. They might have taken her to the ruined castle, that was where we had ridden that day, and Gwyneth or Amelia had asked whether it was accessible by road. The boys had been with us, and they would have memorised the route and ridden Jewel there bareback. I resolved to ride there myself and see if there were any signs of a horse and a Land Rover and trailer. It was merely for my own curiosity. I would go along with Linda's wishes and say nothing. I was sure that one day I would run into Gwyneth and Amelia, and then I would know the truth. Until then, I would let it rest.

THE END

The Engagement Party

During the merry month of May 1964, we imagined that we would enjoy a hiatus of peace in our family home, Blainstock Castle, in the Scottish Highlands. We had recently entertained six prize winners for two action-packed weeks in a competition organised by the magazine *Riding*. Then, my best friend, Ann and her boyfriend, Henry, descended upon us for a flying visit. The recently arrived tenants in the Dower House had settled in and were, more or less, managing their own household and no longer eating their meals at our table. This respite would allow us to gear up for summer and our hoped-for invasion of guests who wanted to enjoy the Highland scenery, trekking and sailing on the loch before the shooting began in August.

Mummy, her husband, Richard, my young half-brother, Hamish, and I sat down to a leisurely breakfast. In the tradition of the best stories, a letter arrived to mark the beginning of an enthralling and disturbing chapter in our lives.

"Oh! My golly gosh!" exclaimed Mummy, who avoided blasphemy and disapproved of taking the Lord's name in vain.

"What is it, Catherine?" asked Richard, who looked up from his perusal of the local newspaper.

"This is from my sister, Primrose," said Mummy, her eyes scanning her letter.

"What's up with Cecilia?" I asked, shaken out of my secret thoughts about whether I might be seeing Frank today. It seemed very likely as he was one of the three tenants of the Dower House. He was the horse trainer of Jack and Yola Laskey and spent a good proportion of his day with their two horses over at the stables.

"Cecilia is engaged," pronounced Mummy.

"Goodness, who on earth would want to marry Cecilia?" I asked.

"Royce Pevensy!" pronounced Mummy triumphantly.

"Jumping Russian rabbits!" I was utterly astonished. I had thought poor dowdy Cecilia might be sitting permanently on a dusty shelf. It had never occurred to me that she would nab a future Duke. "That means she's going to be a Duchess!"

"Yes, indeed," said Mummy. "You've obviously underestimated the charms of your cousin."

"She's going to marry into the premier horsey family in Oxfordshire." An uncomfortable feeling assailed me. I would not admit to actual jealousy or envy, but this would mean that Cecilia was not only shooting up the social scale but, perhaps more significantly, the Oxfordshire equestrian hierarchy. Not that I would admit to being too concerned by such things, but you cannot deny that the British class system exists and affects the way things are. This familial association would link us to the local aristocracy, and I wasn't at all sure I liked the implications.

"Cecilia's accession to the aristocracy will entail a great deal of uncomfortable goodwill imposed upon the innocent tenantry," I said.

"Jill, you sound like you've swallowed a dictionary," commented Richard mildly.

"Don't forget you've married into a literary family," I retorted. "Can you imagine Cecilia playing the Lady of the Manor opening fetes in full panoply?" I had a vision of her in a much-flowered dress, mid-calf length displaying her thickset ankles, with a wide-brimmed straw hat with matching blooms around the brim. Cecilia was large-boned, blonde, with a highly-coloured complexion, taking after her florid and robust father, my Uncle Henry. She would certainly be an imposing figure as a Duchess in full flight.

The Pevensys had recently been linked to several other people in our family and social orbit.

"Does this mean she will be related to Mark Lansdowne if he marries Mercedes?" I asked, whipping the stub of a pencil out of my pocket and drawing diagrams on a page in my little notebook.

Mark Lansdowne is the nephew of my step-father Richard, and he has been in determined pursuit of Mercedes Pevensy, the eldest daughter and second child of the Duke and Duchess of Tolkington. So, if Cecilia were to marry the eldest son and heir, she would be the sister-in-law of Mark.

There were five Pevensy children. The two eldest, Royce and Mercedes, were known as good quality people, thoroughly decent and well respected. The next two, Austin was a Jack the Lad and Porsche, an extremely badly behaved teenage rebel who had been withdrawn from her boarding school and forced to attend the local comprehensive. They were often in cahoots and involved in dastardly schemes. Austin had been carrying on with Susan King, formerly Pyke, with whom I had a longstanding abrasive relationship based on mutual dislike. Susan had been the first of my cohort to marry a boring local solicitor called Bartholomew King, and it hadn't taken her long to bestow her attentions upon Austin, who was, admittedly, an extremely dashing young man. The youngest Pevensy child was Morgan. She was best friends with Lavender Ellison-Heath, the proud owner of Black Boy, my first pony, until her mother sold him. Eventually, as related in *The Adventures of Jill's Ponies*, I had managed to buy back Black Boy, and he was now safely at Blainstock, never to leave again.

"The Pevensys do rather cast their net across our friends and not-so-friends," I mused.

"That is not really the point," said Mummy, divining my less-than-noble thoughts. "The point is that Primrose has asked us to host a sort of engagement house party for a select group of

relatives and friends. She feels that our side of the family must put up a bit of a show of grandeur, and a Scottish castle is just the thing."

"That is a challenge," said Richard.

"She assures us that Henry will foot the bill so that it will be a business proposition. But, I'm not sure that we shouldn't offer to do it for free out of family loyalty," said Mummy.

"Perhaps a substantial discount is in order," said Richard.

"Yes, yes. Of course. This sounds mercenary, but we are still watching the pennies," said Mummy. "I know you saved the day with your donation of £8,000 into the family coffers when you sold your wonderful horse, Jill, but we're not out of the woods yet."

"It would mean that these esteemed Pevensys might spread the word about our castle and Scottish hospitality, and we would attract more guests," said Richard in practical terms. "Mercedes was here as a judge for the competitions of the prize winners, so she knows something of how we operate, and this would be a chance for us to consolidate our reputation."

"Yes, you're right, darling," said Mummy. "Then, you agree that we should host this party. The thing is that it will be rather a rush. The dates that Primrose suggests are the last week in May, so we have only two weeks to prepare."

"How many guests?" I asked. "Presumably, they'll want to ride while they're here."

That would mean some of the business would go to Blainstock Riding Stables, a separate enterprise from the castle. I was an equal quarter owner of the stables, along with John, Linda and Hugh Gillis. We could provide the guests with mounts for trekking.

"We could do a day when we ride to the sea," I said. "That is always a fun expedition."

"Yes, it's interesting," said Mummy. "Cecilia always claimed she could ride, but I understand that you didn't rate her as a horsewoman?"

"She wasn't up to much, but we have any number of quiet mounts that could reliably carry her over the hills. Anyway, I gather that Royce does ride, but he's not horse-mad like Mercedes, Porsche and Austin," I said. "He likes poetry. Was Cecilia keen on poetry?"

"I've never heard of Cecilia being much on poetry. It was collecting wildflowers and embroidery," said Mummy. "I'll ring Primrose this morning and tell her we can certainly do this party. We need numbers and dates, and then we can work out how much it should cost. I'll also get the juicy details about how they got together."

"The last I heard, Royce was pining after a china-doll pretty girl, daughter of a vicar, called Serafina Collins."

"It must have been true love at first sight with Cecilia. And, to get engaged so quickly," said Mummy looking thoughtful. "Just think, Jill. Your cousin is going to be the Duchess of Tolkington one day!"

"When is the wedding?" I asked.

"Not til June next year. A sudden engagement should be followed by a decent length of time before the wedding. Primrose doesn't want scurrilous rumours."

*****

I raced over to the stables as soon as I had finished breakfast. I was there in time to muck out both Balius and Shadow's boxes. I was determined to pull my weight; if nothing else, I would clean out my horses' stables. I thought we might employ a working pupil, or even two, this summer to have some help. We had so many horses at the moment we needed extra help.

I rode Balius first. He was coming on so well. I was determined that we would be showjumping all summer, even if it meant just touring the shows in the north. However, I wasn't sure whether I should spend the summer in Oxfordshire, not with Frank being here in Scotland.

I was schooling him very seriously, as riders do in all the good pony books, and had managed to stop thinking about whether Frank would come over and school one of the Laskey horses.

We were achieving a creditable shoulder-in down the long side when I saw Balius's sensitive ears flicker. Another horse had entered the arena. I looked over, hopefully, and saw that it was Yola on Skydiver. She had every right to school the horse that now belonged to her in the indoor school. She had certainly paid handsomely for the privilege. Then I saw that Frank was walking behind her. As her horse trainer, he would be assisting her in her training. One had to admit she needed all the assistance she could get.

She might think that she was a wonderful rider, and perhaps by American dressage standards, she was. But she had a long way to go before she could hold her own on the European circuit, which was her ambition. Her dressage horse, Skydiver, was an extraordinary animal. I had bought him from De Luxe Movie Horses, and he had proved himself almost bombproof. He could perform the most accomplished movements with the sketchiest of aids. Each of the prize winners had had to ride him in an advanced test as one of their small competitions, and he had shown himself as easy-going and adaptable no matter which rider was on him. His one quirk was that he was terrified of thunderstorms, and riding during a storm was to be avoided if at all possible.

Of course, I hadn't wanted to sell him, particularly to the unlikeable Yola, who was married to the extremely unlikeable Jack Laskey. Still, they had offered me £20,000, which had pulled us back from the brink of insolvency. Anyway, I had got over my obsession with dressage and found that I preferred showjumping which had always been my favourite thing as a teenager. Frank was a keen showjumper.

I rode up to the far end of the arena to give Yola room to do her schooling and practised some small circles called voltes. Balius was getting much more balanced and flexible these days, and I wanted to be able to turn him quickly if we got to the jump-off in a showjumping competition. I didn't sit and stare at Yola and Skydiver, but as I rode out of the arena, I noticed that Frank was trying to help her improve her sitting trot. I couldn't help but wince as I saw her bumping inelegantly on poor Skydiver's back and hoped that he wasn't going to suffer permanent damage.

I got back to the stables and rubbed down Balius. He was whiffling away, and I produced two sugar lumps which I had taken from the sugar bowl on the breakfast table. The weather was divinely spring-like, and I decided he could do without a rug and let him go up the hill in one of the small walled fields.

I went back to the stables and tacked up Shadow. He was one year older than Balius, his full brother, but only recently broken in. He was still a novice but showed huge promise. Slightly smaller than Balius, he was more finely set. They were both one-quarter Highland pony and three-quarters thoroughbred. I couldn't bear to go back to the indoor shool and took him to the outdoor arena, where we had some showjumps.

I warmed him up for at least twenty minutes, walking and then trotting on a long rein. Then, gathering him together, I tried some twenty-metre circles and then fifteen-metre circles, first trotting and then cantering. He seemed to enjoy his work, and I decided we would jump the half-dozen small jumps, that would be sufficient for him. He bounced over each of the jumps, none higher than two feet-nine inches, and then I decided that a quick circuit of the loch might be nice on such a glorious morning.

Richard was in his small boat skimming across the wavelets. I gave him a cheery wave, and we set off at a steady canter around the broad sandy track that encircled our loch. The prospect of the engagement party was certainly intriguing. I vaguely remembered meeting Royce once, and he had seemed a decent chap, reserved and exceedingly polite. He would probably make an excellent husband, and I was pleased for my cousin, who had always been a little odd. Although, to be fair, she probably classified me as strange with my obsession with ponies and now horses.

I walked the last half mile home, and after rubbing down Shadow and giving him two lumps of sugar, I put him in the small field with Balius. They were a wonderful sight, so similar but not quite. Then I hurried back to the house, curious about Mummy's phone call to Aunt Primrose.

By now, Jack Laskey, obviously not an early riser, was riding Firestorm in the outdoor arena. He was Yola's husband. Devoted readers might remember him as an instructor at Porlock Vale when I went there to become a qualified riding instructor. Yes, I admit, he was a man I had once been infatuated with, and then I realised what a tricky dicky he was.

Since then, I have become more worldly and realised that it was just 'the older man routine'. It's one of the things that you have to go through, like teething. A short while ago, he and Yola had turned up as our tenants. I hadn't been pleased as I didn't like being reminded of my youthful foolish infatuation. But they were paying us a handsome rent for the Dower House, and I had to concentrate on the Greater Good, which was our finances.

Their horse trainer, Frank Stabley, was the man who had taken me out on my only date. It had been a cheerful visit to a local Italian restaurant concluding with a chaste kiss. Then Frank had flown off to America, and I had departed for Australia. Now, I realised that I did have some rather uncomfortable thoughts about Frank, but I was determined that as all my other female friends and acquaintances, and now even Cecilia, were indulging in the great game of finding a husband, I should grasp the nettle. Frank was a few years older than me, a showjumper who I had seen around the shows in my teenage years. He was a thoroughly decent chap, and now I'd got to know him a little more, I realised how witty and clever he was. He had a keen eye for the vagaries of human nature, and we seemed to share the same sense of humour. And more importantly, he was a very good rider and had a way with horses.

*****

At lunch, Mummy was bubbling over with news. She had had a long conversation with Aunt Primrose.

"Oh, Jill! The tale I have to tell! Primrose was full of it. She is tremendously excited at the prospect of being related by marriage to the Duke and Duchess. You know she has always longed to mix with the great and the good, and now her daughter is to be a Duchess."

"How thrilling for her," I pronounced dryly. "How did it all come about?"

"Jill, you're not jealous?" asked Mummy.

I snorted. One of those magnificent snorts that express one's feelings far more clearly than an exclamation.

"Don't make that noise, darling. It is not at all ladylike," commented Mummy mildly.

"Come on, don't keep me in suspenders. How did it all come about?" I asked impatiently.

"Cecilia was heavily involved in local good works, and she and Aggie Pevensy were organising a Bring and Buy Sale to raise funds for the Langton Shrove church. Apparently, there was some talk of the wedding being held there, but now it's been decided that the cathedral in Oxford will be more the thing."

"The thing," I echoed. "We must always consider 'the thing'."

"Anyway, Cecilia and Aggie were kindred spirits, and the Duchess took your cousin under her wing. Unfortunately, it appears that Royce had developed an unrequited passion for a young woman called Serafina, a horrid, artificial creature whose father was a Vicar in Oxford. Aggie disapproved of her and thought her a scheming minx. Anyway, she was much too glamorous for Royce, who is a farmer to the core. So, Aggie introduced Cecilia to bustle him out of his megrims."

Privately, I thought that a constant dose of Cecilia might drive one into the pits of despair, but it appears not in the case of Royce. Aggie was a formidable matriarch, a force of nature, and as she had decided that Cecilia's managing nature and gusto for good works was just what she needed for the next Duchess, there was no doubt that it would come about.

"Royce bucked up no end, and between them, his mother and Cecilia brought him to the point of a proposal. So, there it is!"

"Good old Cecilia. I am honestly pleased for her," I said nobly.

"It seems Aggie is already arranging for Cecilia to join the Parish Council, and she's got her involved in every good work within a twenty-mile radius of Shrove Langton."

"Poor Cecilia, how dreary," I sympathised. "But I suppose it's right up her alley, so all's well that ends well."

"This party will include a rather large gathering, and Primrose wants us to row the boat out, so to speak. We're to plan for every type of entertainment we can think of. Five-course dinners and a gala fancy dress dance on Saturday night, with a band coming up from Edinburgh. I told her that Frank Stabley was here, and she's insisted that he join the fray as he's a Chatton boy with some acquaintance with Cecilia. Including Richard and me, you and Frank, that makes about twenty-four or so. Ann and Henry are invited, and this will make you laugh, Susan and Barty King."

"What about Jack and Yola Laskey?" I asked. "If we invite Frank to join the jamboree, it will be awkward to exclude them?"

"Yes, I see what you mean. I'll talk to Richard about it," said Mummy frowning. "That could be rather tricky."

"We'll have to think of fancy dress costumes for ourselves, and then I had a bright idea. If we were to put together a collection of such outfits, we could do the same thing ourselves for our guests, and in the future, they could choose costumes from our collection when they're staying here."

"That's a clever idea," said Richard, who, up until that point, had been quietly munching his way through a very tasty piece of cold veal pie.

"Do you remember I found those two big old trunks in the attic?" I said, struck with inspiration. "They were chocka-bloc full of old clothes. We could haul them down and have a look in there."

"Jill, you're a brain box!" declared Mummy. "Richard, can you get one of the men to help you and haul them down? We can put them in that box room at the end of the guest corridor."

"Of course, my dear," said Richard obligingly.

"As well as fancy dress, there's horse riding, of course. We can probably mount anyone who wants to ride," I said, my mind running to how the stables might profit.

"Yes, and sailing on the loch. I'm happy to organise for anyone who might want to go boating," said Richard. "And fishing as well. And, if the weather turns against us then there is the games room."

"And," I continued in a fit of daring, "there is always the television."

Silence greeted this statement. In the fifties television was considered to be a lowly form of entertainment only for the servant classes. The gentry thought that there was something unpleasantly egalitarian about the box. In the heady years of the early 1960s, entertainment for the masses was considered more acceptable, even to those with social pretensions. My film star friend Beau Carlisle had recently accepted a big role in a BBC drama. Previously, no actor worth his salt would have appeared in an advertisement or on television, but Beau had declared that television was the future and he would be at the forefront.

I rang Ann that night. Blow the expense.

"I'll pay out of my own money," I assured Mummy. "This is just too delicious a topic to miss a good heart-to-heart."

Ann, of course, knew all about it. I would have been disappointed if I had thought I would surprise her. News goes around Chatton like the black death.

"Oh, yes! Yes! And the engagement party is to be at the castle."

"Have you got your invitation?" I asked.

"Not yet. We're waiting with bated breath to see if it arrives in the post."

"Well, according to Aunt Primrose, you and Henry are on the list. And get this! Also, Susan and Barty King!"

"I ran into Wendy Mead at Mrs Buzzby's shop, and she was full of it. It's the talk of the County. She wishes she might be invited but hardly knows Cecilia, so she doubts it. Do tell! How on earth did Cecilia and Royce get together?"

"They met through Cecilia doing good works, and Aggie spotted her potential as a future Duchess and organised it," I replied.

"How many children do you think they'll have?" asked Ann.

"Cecilia can be quite religious, you know. She may take the Biblical injunction to heart and go out and multiply."

"They'll need an heir and a spare, at least," said Ann.

"Once they have children, there's no hope that the Dukedom shall go to Austin," I mused. "Are he and Susan still special friends? That could be very awkward with Barty coming to the castle with her."

Ann immediately cottoned on to what I was saying. Susan had been shamelessly running around with Austin even though she was married to a dull stick, Bartholomew King, a local solicitor. None of us could ever understand why she had married him. If he had been inordinately wealthy, then it would have been a simple case of Bride Sacrifice, but he was neither rich nor charming.

"That's all over now," said Ann. "Austin has been seen parading around with another, the Hon Rosemary Dill. There have even been rumours of a double wedding, although I believe that is considered rather *infra dig*. Anyway, Austin hasn't come to the point. You'll be able to suss it out when they come to the party at the castle. Austin will be sure to be there with this Rosemary. From what I gather, Aggie is promoting the match. Although, I don't think Austin will be as compliant as Royce in going along with his mother's matrimonial ideas."

"Poor old Susan," I said with genuine pity. "I'm sure she dreamed of quietly divorcing Barty and being wed to that rat, Austin."

"I imagine she'll be taking it rather hard," said Ann. "Cecilia will probably want you as a bridesmaid."

"That will be utterly gruesome," I groaned. "Can you imagine the bows and furbelows that Cecilia will choose?"

"Perhaps Aggie will step in and ensure that it's all in good taste," said Ann. "I don't envy Cecilia, her future mother-in-law."

It struck me then that Ann had never mentioned anything about her boyfriend's family.

"What is Henry's mother like?" I asked.

"Arrh," said Ann. "That's a topic for a much longer chat, face-to-face."

"That sounds utterly intriguing. I see we'll have to talk seriously when you get here."

"I wouldn't miss it in a hundred years," said Ann. "We'll make time, I can assure you."

*****

Several days later, a large packet from Aunt Primrose arrived in the post. There were twenty-two guests, including the happy couple, Aunt Primrose and Uncle Henry, and the Duke and Duchess. That didn't include those of us who lived at Blainstock.

"Who on earth has the surname Dill?" I commented to Mummy, scanning the guest list.

"It's an important family who've been closely associated with the Royals for generations," said Mummy. "Let's be systematic with this. Six oldies are me and Richard, Primrose and Henry, and Aggie and Louis. Then, there are two youngsters. Oh, look, Jill! Little Lavender Ellison-Heath and Morgan Pevensy, she must be the youngest child."

"Lavender will love being able to see Black Boy again," I commented.

"Then, there's the happy couple, Cecilia and Royce. There's you, Frank, Ann, Henry, Susan and Barty King on Cecilia's side."

"Surely, Cecilia has invited Clarissa, who-used-to-be Dandleby?" I questioned. "She was one of Cecilia's best friends. Perhaps, her marriage to that old bloke Charlie Moreton makes her socially unsuitable."

"On Royce's side, we've got Mercedes, but no Mark?" said Mummy.

"Does that mean they've split up, or Mark has made excuses because he hates coming here?" I pondered. Mark Lansdowne was my stepfather's nephew, and he and I did not get on.

"I have no idea, but I'm sure you'll make enquiries and discover the situation," said Mummy.

"There's Austin, and this must be his new girlfriend the Hon Rosemary Dill. Here's Ernest Shipton-Hill and Serafina Collins. That would be the girl that Royce had been keen on. She's ended up with one of his friends." Mummy frowned over the list.

"Jill! This is going to be interesting, a Simon Caxton-Thorpe, yet another double-barrelled name, and his partner is Dinah Dean!"

"Gosh! I thought Dinah's socialist ideals would not permit her to stoop to consorting with the upper classes!" I exclaimed.

"Perhaps true love has hit her," said Mummy. "Or she is converting Simon to her political line of thought. Then there's a single man, Theodore Chapman, and another couple, Buster and Gertrude Scobie, one more Bunty Pope, and a man called Chumley."

"They don't sound like they're going to fit in with the rest," I said. "Salt of the earth, perhaps?"

"We shall meet them all soon enough," said Mummy. "Here is the proposed timetable of events. They arrive on Thursday afternoon or evening. Some are coming by train, and others are driving up. A buffet supper so people can eat after they have unpacked, and that will be more convenient for latecomers.

"Then, on Friday, it is suggested that some might like to ride, sail on the loch, lie around in the gardens, or walk. A sit-down dinner on Friday night in formal dress. Primrose has even included a diagram of place settings.

"Then Saturday night is the fancy dress. Perhaps some guests might want to drive into Aberdeen, see the sights, and buy costumes if they have forgotten. And another opportunity to ride. Maybe a ride to the sea might be a good idea.

"Sunday morning will be church service at Craigie. Traditional Sunday lunch and more riding, walking or boating."

"That sounds achievable," I said. "Nothing we haven't done before, except for the fancy dress. We'll have to sort out our own outfits. I might ring Ann and see what she plans for herself and Henry."

"Yes, dear. I need to talk to Cook, and we'll do the menus and then the shopping list. She'll have to arrange extra help from the village."

I went over to the stables to talk to Linda, Hugh and John. They were mucking out and I leapt in to help.

"The ride to the sea on Saturday is awkward," said Linda. "It's my busiest day with the riding school."

"Perhaps, some of them can come with us. Do a day ride. By the way, Lavender is coming up, so Black Boy must be reserved for her and a pony for Morgan Pevensy. She's a capable rider but not keen. Which one do you think?"

"Well, Bonnie might be needed for some of the less able adult riders, also Copperplate and the bigger ponies. Perhaps Morgan can ride Rex?"

"I suppose so," I said. "She might not even want to ride. But if Lavender is riding, then she will probably tag along too. Imagine how Ann and I would have loved to come up here when we were that age!"

"Let's hope they don't all want to ride at once, as we probably won't have enough horses."

"I suppose some will go walking or boating on the loch. Royce is rather keen on poetry and so are his best friends. They might sit in the garden and do recitations," I said hesitantly. I wasn't sure what poetic people actually did with their poetry.

"They might have a writing thing. You know where they all come up with rhymes and things together," said John.

"You know that might be a possible week you could do. A writer's workshop. You and your mother should know some literary types, or at least where to advertise," said Hugh.

"I suppose that might work," I said.

At that point, Jack, Yola and Frank strolled into the stable yard.

"I'm going to jump Firestorm this morning in the outside arena," announced Jack to the world at large.

"John and I can come over and set up the jumps if you like," said Hugh. He was always assiduously polite to Jack and Yola, showing how much he disliked them.

"I might hang around and watch," I said. I wanted to talk to Frank. Perhaps Aunt Primrose would send him a formal invitation, but I would warn him he was to join the party. I didn't think it was tactful to say anything in front of Jack and Yola. It would be unrealistic for the Laskeys to be invited, neither of them had ever met Royce or Cecilia, but it was also a little awkward. They would have to understand that it was a private party but that Frank had known many of the guests all his life.

Firestorm was a massive horse, over 17 hh, fiery and difficult to ride with a huge bouncy stride. He danced around as if he were on gigantic springs, going up and down like an erratic yo-yo. He used to belong to Mark Lansdowne, and then his ownership was transferred to Blainstock Riding Stables. Linda had cleverly managed to palm him off on Jack, and now the two of them were battling it out, each attempting to be the boss of the other. They were both dominant personalities. Although Firestorm appreciated having a rider who knew what they were doing and could control his pace and position him in front of the jumps, he liked to be treated respectfully. A tactful hand was needed to control him. Jack was not tactful, and he liked to be seen to be in charge.

"I want the jumps to be set at four-feet and four-feet six," he instructed Hugh and John. They set them up accordingly. A double with two big strides between the elements on one side of the arena and on the other, three jumps, with five and a half strides between the first and the second and six and a half strides to the third. Then, a triple bar at the end of the arena. It was wider than it was high. And a wonderful wall that had been painted with two different landscapes on either side.

Lettie Lonsdale had designed it, with the help of Rennie Jordan, as one of the competitions for the prize winners. It was almost too artistic to use as a jump, but John had layered it in varnish so the paintwork wouldn't get faded and chipped. On one side was a painted scene of a beautiful river with swans and the cutest little crooked cottage, and on the other was the castle with the mountains in the distance.

Frank hurried over and talked to Jack. He was their horse trainer, thus, it was his duty to make suggestions. Jack paid him scant attention. He treated Frank more as a dogsbody and

an instructor for Yola and Skydiver when they were doing their dressage. Frank came back to stand next to me. Yola was talking to Linda about Skydiver.

"You know my cousin, Cecilia," I said to Frank.

"Yes, vaguely. She didn't ride at the shows, though," he replied.

"She's having an engagement party up here in a couple of weeks. She's marrying Royce Pevensy. Her mother, my Aunt Primrose, suggested that you might like to join the party. It starts on Thursday evening, and there is a formal dinner on Friday night and a fancy dress ball on Saturday. Ann and Henry, and Susan and Barty King are coming. And Dinah Dean, she's the girlfriend of one of Royce's friends."

"That's a sizeable contingent from Chatton," remarked Frank. "I would love to join you. I might just have to clear it with Jack and Yola. I suppose I could take a few days of leave. I'm due some time off."

"The fancy dress is going to be fun," I said. "I've never dressed up in a costume before. What do you reckon?"

He looked thoughtful.

"I can't think of anything off the top of my head," he replied. He didn't suggest that we dress up as a pair.

Jack and Firestorm bucketed into the arena. The big chestnut gelding was looking at the jumps, his eyes bulging with excitement. Jack seemed to be doing his best to hot him up, needling his sides with blunt spurs and pulling on the reins, bending his neck to one side and then the other. They cantered around the arena. Firestorm had a big, bouncy stride at the best of times, and I had to admit that Jack sat him admirably. He only circled the arena three times in either direction, which seemed an insufficient warm-up to me. They bounded towards the double. Firestorm had a huge jump in him, but he was impetuous, and it didn't help when he was over-excited. They leapt the first element, and then although it was two long strides to the second, they came in too close. Firestorm's front legs crashed the top rail.

Frank ran in to put up the pole. Jack lashed Firestorm with his whip, one slash on either side of his flanks. Such treatment was totally unnecessary. They wouldn't have gotten in so close if Jack had controlled his speed more accurately. I opened my mouth to say something, then shut it. I couldn't bear to watch this. I turned on my heel and walked away. After that, I would school Balius in the indoor arena. It made me more determined than ever to finesse my riding and train Balius to approach any jump with just the right amount of pace and impulsion at different angles. I had been thinking about jump-offs recently and decided that to be able to jump at an angle would help us achieve faster times.

*****

That afternoon Mummy and I got together and racked our brains to come up with some good costume ideas for our planned trunk of outfits that could be used for future house parties.

"I've made a list," said Mummy. "I've got a tramp, a Japanese kimono, a clown, 1920s flapper outfit, and I haven't got much further."

I groaned. I couldn't think of a thing. "I suppose a tramp would be good if someone hasn't brought a costume. I'm not much of a fan of this sort of activity. It seems frivolous and pointless. I suppose there's always the old toga."

"I must look out for a supply of old sheets. I don't want the guests purloining our best linen," said Mummy. "I can see it from your point of view. Perhaps on some deeper level, it is being something other than one's ordinary self. A disguise in which to reveal a deeper hidden part of yourself. I've just had an inspiration. Don't worry about your costume Jill. I will organise it for you, and it will be a surprise on the night."

I frowned. Did I have some mysterious deeper self that Mummy was determined should be revealed? I wasn't sure that I liked surprises like that, but it was good of Mummy to take the onerous task of devising a costume out of my hands.

"Did Aunt Primrose mention what Cecilia and Royce might be dressing up as?"

"Cecilia is deep into a project now, creating some very elaborate French aristocratic outfits that might have been in the times of Marie Antoinette."

"Off with her head," I quipped. "Do you think that is what Cecilia envisages as her future role? Someone who treats the peasants as if they were less than dust."

"I don't think so. She seems very serious-minded regarding helping the poor," said Mummy.

"Perhaps she'll throw us a few shekels if the castle business doesn't succeed," I said sardonically, my mouth twisted in a crooked smile.

"I wouldn't want to be an object of charity for my relatives," said Mummy huffily. She had always managed to support us by writing children's books before she married Richard. "Anyway, my publisher is very pleased with the children's book that Arleen and I have concocted. He is talking about a series."

"What about Aunt Primrose and Uncle Henry? Are they getting dressed up?"

"Primrose said they had no choice but to aim for something conservative. So you can imagine your corpulent uncle in some fancy outfit!"

"I wonder what the Duke and Duchess will appear as?"

"Something a little more outrageous, I imagine," said Mummy. "This engagement party will be rather interesting from start to finish."

At that point, we had no idea just how interesting!

*****

The next two weeks flashed by at the speed of light. I was disappointed that when I had told Frank about the fancy dress, he hadn't come back to me with the suggestion that we dress up in matching costumes. That was another knotty issue. Most of the guests were pairs. I wasn't sure if it was

Frank and Jill at this point. In fact, the whole Frank and me question was gnawing away at me like a rat chewing on an old bone. Nothing was said between us. There were a few long lingering looks on both sides, or so I thought, but my experience in the romance department was zero, a big fat nought. I remembered that Frank had once taken out Serena, the riding instructor at Mrs Darcy's riding school. He was the one who had done this 'going out' thing before. As far as I was concerned, it was up to him to lead the way. Then again, perhaps it was entirely my imagination, and he saw me as nothing but a friend who he had known for many years.

On Thursday, when the guests were due to arrive, Ann and Henry tootled up the drive first. They had left Chatton two days ago and stayed overnight at Carlisle.

"I don't want to miss a minute of this event. It promises to be vastly entertaining," said Ann merrily.

"You haven't been knee-deep in preparations for the last two weeks," I said. "How about we go out for a ride before the rest of them arrive? "

"Wonderful. I could do with some fresh Highland air after sitting in the car for so long," replied Ann. "Henry, would you like to ride?"

"Certainly," said the ever-obliging Henry.

"Perhaps Frank can come too. I want to ride Copperplate again. She is the most darling sweet mare," said Ann.

"Of course, you can have your pick. Henry, would you like to ride Balius? I'll be on Shadow, and perhaps Frank can ride Rumble again. I'm not sure what Linda is up to with him," I said.

Rumble was a good-looking and promising thoroughbred that Linda and Hugh had bought from a sale down south. He was a prospect for Linda to compete on, and she had been riding him a lot, but I hadn't seen how he was going.

I dashed over to the Dower House, hoping that Jack and Yola wouldn't be around. Frank was in the laundry, cleaning boots.

"Gosh, I didn't realise you had to be an actual servant," I exclaimed tactlessly.

"We can't ask the girls from the village to do this sort of work. I think that Jack and Yola imagine that boots just magically clean themselves," said Frank cheerfully. I regretted my remark about him being a servant. I didn't want him to think I was getting uppity.

"Ann and Henry have arrived. Do you want to come out for a ride with us?"

"Yes, that would be good. Catch up with news from Chatton," he replied easily.

"Ann is riding Copperplate, Henry on Balius and me on Shadow."

"Jack and Yola went off to Edinburgh for a few days this morning so that I might take Skydiver out. He's been trotting around the arena carrying Yola for days now. It would be good to go out with the others and let him be an ordinary horse for a while," replied Frank.

Ann and Henry had taken their bags upstairs. Ann was with me in my turret room, and Henry had been given one of the guest rooms.

"At least I know with Ann and Henry they're not sharing a bed," said Mummy. I'm not sure what the arrangement is for the other couples. For example, are Ernest and Serafina in one room, Simon and Dinah Dean, and Austin and Rosemary? I know that young people are much more free-and-easy these days, but Primrose gave me no instructions. I suppose we caput them in separate rooms, and they can creep along the corridors in the middle of the night if that is what they want."

I hadn't even given these things a thought, which shows just how naïve and unaccustomed to the ways of the modern world I was. My mind went into overdrive, and I imagined all these young people swooning over each other. Perhaps we would find bodies all over the place, having passionate scenes in the most awkward locations, in cupboards, on the stairs, or behind the curtains.

"Gosh! Don't ask me," I said, my mind veering away from such a tricky subject. "We're all going out for a ride. I'll leave the logistics of putting people in beds to you. You're much more tactful and considerate. I would just mess it up."

"Yes, dear. You go and ride," said Mummy soothingly. "The Pevensys and the Talbots are arriving by train, so Richard and Hugh are picking them up from the station at about two o'clock. They're a party of twelve, so it will be a few trips. I imagine mountains of luggage."

"Let's get away from the onrush of guests," I said to Ann and Henry, and we dashed over to the stables.

"That Skydiver really is a magnificent horse," said Henry, watching Frank ride beside him as we set out up the track that led between the small stone-walled fields.

"Even when he is in the paddock, he prances around. Seems to practise elegant and extravagant movements on his own. Always the same, no matter who has been riding him," said Frank, alluding to the inept Yola.

"Shadow is coming on wonderfully," I said, changing the subject. It still rankled that I had had to sell Skydiver to the Laskeys. They had offered just too much money to turn down, especially considering we had been on the brink of bankruptcy since Richard's crooked lawyer had run off with the family trust. "I think I might be able to take him in some novice hack and riding classes this summer, to give him some experience of shows, other horses, the hustle and bustle."

"And you were saying that Balius is more than ready for the fray," said Ann. "Open jumping classes at the smaller shows and Foxhunter at the bigger ones."

"I'll have to become a member of the BSJA for that," I said. "I'm not sure how much I'll have to be at Blainstock this summer and how much time free for gallivanting around the shows."

"At least your summer is going to be full of horse riding, no matter which way it goes," said Henry. "I'm finding myself spending at least half my time in cow sheds and pig sties."

We came to the track around the loch and set off at a sedate canter. Skydiver was in the lead, tossing his head and snuffing the air. Frank let him go on a long rein and choose his own stride, and he seemed to appreciate this gesture.

There were thin white streamers of cloud streaking across the blue sky. The mountains were clearly etched on the horizon, and the hillsides were ablaze with golden gorse.

"This is the most glorious countryside," said Ann. "I don't think I would ever tire of the vistas."

"Yes, but sometimes I miss the green fields and little lanes of Oxfordshire," I replied.

"I've heard that once you've lived in two different places, you never quite feel at home in either," said Henry.

I knew that the plan had been for Ann to move to Bristol to study veterinary medicine at university there, and Henry had thought to go with her. I had asked her a few times about her plans in that direction, but she had shrugged it off, saying that she had to see whether or not she had done well enough to gain university entrance. She never brought up the subject herself, and I wondered if she was still as keen.

"What about you, Frank? Are you longing to get back to Oxfordshire? You've been away for a while now, first America and now Scotland?" asked Ann.

"I'm happy enough up here for now," said Frank. "Of course, I won't work for Jack and Yola forever. Eventually, I'll return to the farm with Dad and do my showjumping thing."

This gave me food for thought. I would never have expected Frank to stay up here forever. If we did get together, and that was a big 'if', that would mean going back to Oxfordshire. It would also mean leaving Blainstock Riding Stables, not that Hugh, Linda and John couldn't run it perfectly well without me. It was all too confusing. This trying to figure out where we should all be as we inevitably settled down. It made me feel like heading off to foreign shores again just so I didn't have to face that inevitable growing-up thing.

"Let's go up this track," I said, diverting myself from such disturbing thoughts. "The view from the top is rather good, and some uphill work will help to build up the horses' muscles."

"They'll be as agile as mountain goats," commented Henry.

We trotted up the narrow track until it became too stony and twisty, and then the horses walked, their heads low, watching the ground so they didn't stumble. The smell of gorse was intoxicating.

"It's all wild hills and rough, uneven ways," said Henry.

We dismounted when we got to the top and surveyed the scene.

"The emptiness is almost overpowering," said Henry. "Not a habitation in sight. It helps to put our petty human concerns into perspective."

I had the feeling that there was a problem in his life with which he was wrestling. Perhaps it was related to Ann going to Bristol. I would have to get it out of her tonight. Once Ann and I were tucked up into our beds, with the ancient tapestries hung around the turret walls encircling us, it would be the time for confidences.

*****

We returned to the stable yard and set to rubbing down the horses and putting them away in their loose boxes.

"I'm going to bring in Firestorm and lunge him before he's settled for the evening," said Frank. "I'm giving myself a holiday from having to ride him."

"I don't blame you," I said. "We'll have to gird our loins and get back and face the barrage of social activities."

"You sound like you'd rather ride away and camp the night in a remote croft with only candlelight," said Ann.

"You know me too well," I replied.

The twelve-person Pevensy and Talbot contingent had arrived and thronged the corridors and hallways.

I wondered how Cecilia would wear the mantle of a duchess when the time came for her to step up. Although Aggie was such a powerhouse, it was difficult to imagine her retiring gracefully as dowager duchess if Louis passed on before her.

The first thing I noticed about Cecilia was not an ineffable change in her demeanour, but the magnificent three-string pearl necklace around her neck. This was undoubtedly the famous Pevensy pearls. Her engagement ring was positively gaudy, with an unusual design of several bright green emeralds surrounding an enormous diamond.

"Congratulations, cuzz," I said gruffly, feeling surprisingly emotional. The last time I saw her, she was lamenting that life was passing her by. Now she was caught in the grip of a tremendous drama, and she was centre stage.

Cecilia gave me a bear hug. Such an emotional and tactile display on both our sides was a first experience. I hastily turned my attention to the other guests.

The Duke and Duchess processed informally through the hall. Mummy greeted them warmly and led them to the drawing room for a drink to help them get over the stress of the journey. Cecilia and Royce followed behind. Then, Aunt Primrose and Uncle Henry entered, having panted up the front steps, carrying heavy suitcases.

"Oh, you should have left them. Tim would have carried the baggage," I said. "Let me take you through to the drawing room. Leave the suitcases there, and I'll get someone to take them upstairs."

"This place is magnificent," said Aunt Primrose wonderingly. "We should have come up earlier."

Privately, I wondered why they hadn't. If it had been me, I would have been panting with curiosity. Perhaps we hadn't invited them? That was an uncomfortable thought.

The three adult couples sipped on gin and tonics and made polite conversation. I knew that Mummy had been intensely interested in meeting the Pevensys. She had been debating whether or not a curtsey was in order. I told her I thought not.

There was a young man with a pudding bowl haircut and round face with blackcurrant eyes. His manner was exceedingly hearty. I wondered whether he was Royce or Cecilia's friend. Perhaps a former boyfriend. He had latched on to Ann and Henry and were dogging their footsteps. Ann didn't seem to mind. I drew her aside.

"Do you know who he is?" I asked.

"I wouldn't have thought he was your type?" joked Ann.

"I'm not sure he is anybody's type," I retorted unkindly.

"Chumly used to escort Cecilia to various events. His mother is an old friend of Cecilia's mother. I feel sorry for him, but I'm sure there's someone for everyone. Let me introduce you," said Ann with a merry, teasing grin.

Cecilia was in the drawing room with her parents, the Duke and the Duchess.

"Oh, Jill, the young maiden of the castle," said Aggie. "How do you do? Please do call me Aggie, and I'm not sure if you've met my husband, Louis."

That settled the naming issue. Aggie was adroit when it came to ironing out the wrinkles and difficulties of social situations.

"Jill, I absolutely adore this castle. I can't think why I haven't visited before," said Cecilia. I felt guilty for my lack of family feeling. The least we could have done was have Cecilia up here to visit. I resolved to be more thoughtful in the future.

"Jill!" exclaimed a childish voice in the doorway. In skipped Lavender Ellison-Heath. "Can I go over and see Black Boy? I've missed him so much."

"Of course," I replied. "He's been reserved for your exclusive use while you're up here. He's very happy, you know. Some riding school children ride him, just enough to keep life interesting but not too much to be tiresome for him."

"Hello, Morgan," I said. "Are you going to be riding this weekend?"

Morgan, the youngest daughter of Aggie and Louis, shot a meaningful look at her mother. The fact that she didn't like riding had been a bone of contention for some time.

"I don't mind," she shrugged. "I suppose it's a convenient way of looking at the countryside."

"Better than walking," I agreed tactfully. "We thought we might have a ride to the sea on Saturday if you're interested. Some of the riding school kids are booked. It should be fun!"

"Could we swim?" asked Lavender.

"If you're brave enough, but the water will be cold. Nothing like the seaside in Australia, where the water is deliciously fresh in the hot weather," I replied.

"Oh, Australia! How was your trip?" asked Lavender.

"Amazing," I said. "It is so different there, dry and hot, endless empty landscapes, and the people are so casual and friendly."

I didn't say anything about the fact that I had met my long-lost father. Throughout my childhood, I had believed that he was dead. Really, he had been serving a long prison sentence for murder, and Mummy had only revealed the truth before I had left for Australia. He had moved therewhen he was released. But that is another story to be told in my book, *Jill and the Wild Horses*.

"Do you want me to take you to the stables before dinner?" I asked.

"Oh yes! Please!" said Lavender clasping her hands together. "Let's go."

*****

When we got back to the castle, there had been more arrivals. Several carloads of guests had driven in. A long-bonneted black Bentley with seating room for at least ten people was parked on the driveway. There had been five people and all their luggage comfortably stowed: Ernest Shipton-Hill and the very dainty Serafina Collins, Simon Caxton-Thorpe and Dinah Dean, and Rosemary Dill.

I was fascinated by Dinah Dean. As a child, she had been a wild one. She had stolen some horses that were to be sold for meat and lived with them in the forest, sleeping in the roots of a tree. Secretly, I had helped her. I had not openly supported her in those days because I had been afraid of public opinion. I was not proud of myself in that regard. It turned out that Dinah was tremendously intelligent. Mrs Whirtley had taken her under her wing and arranged for her to go to boarding school. Somehow, Dinah's childhood obsession with horses had been put to one side, and she had taken up various causes, such as anti-blood sports and the championing of the poor and underprivileged. She was studying law at Cambridge University.

Now, here she was, the putative girlfriend of Simon Caxton-Thorpe. She had grown up into a strikingly attractive, tall and willowy young woman. The flash of intelligence in her eyes was undeniable. Yet, there was something seductively direct in her gaze, sparkling with ironies and unspoken ideas. She had become one of those people with a special aura, like a comet that leaves a white trail behind as it streaks across the sky. Her consort, Simon, was tall, almost gaunt, pale-skinned with shiny black hair and large, intelligent eyes. He had all the pathos and quick humour of his Celtic ancestors.

"Good evening, Dinah," I said. "I'm Jill Crewe," I said to her partner. "I assume that you're Simon."

"How do you do," he said in a perfectly cultured top-hat accent faintly laced with an Irish lilt. He smiled winsomely, with a hint of a mischievous leprechaun, his grey eyes framed with thick black lashes.

"How did you two meet?" I asked, unable to suppress my curiosity.

"Simon was at Oxford, and we have mutual friends. Now, he is writing poetry. He has a small volume being published shortly," said Dinah with a note of pride in her voice, an unaccustomed softness in her eyes.

"Self-published," added Simon. "Pure vanity, not like you, Jill. Dinah has told me that you are a celebrated scribe with a prodigious literary output."

"I can't imagine writing poetry," I said. "Mine is more like social comedy with lots of horse and pony characters."

"Well, poetry is playing with words and ideas. Not like you, creating a whole world of characters and adventures," said Simon.

"Yes, but inspired by my life," I replied.

"I would be honoured to make an appearance in your literary output," said Simon.

He was so endearingly polite and sweet. I thought he was the perfect foil for Dinah's utterly determined and ruthless pursuit of what is right and honourable.

"I don't know why you don't try writing something more serious, Jill," said Dinah, "your work is so light it might just float away like candy floss. If you set your mind to it, did some serious reading of Proust, Dostoevsky, or even George Eliot, it might help to reshape your style."

"I like to keep away from high literature in case it puts me off my stroke," I said loftily.

"Let me introduce you to Ernest and Serafina," said Simon, trying to rescue us from the social awkwardness created by Dinah's suggestion. "Ernest is also a poet. We formed a poet's society with Royce when we were up at Oxford."

"We were bound together in existential angst," said Ernest in a mocking self-deprecating manner.

"Hello, Serafina," said Ann, dragging Henry by the hand to come over and join the group. "Do you remember we met at the Pevensy Christmas party?"

"Yes, of course," said Serafina, smiling insincerely.

"Henry, this is Serafina. I'm Ann Derry," said Ann, smiling brightly at Ernest.

"Ernest, Ann and Henry," I said, trying to fulfil my hostess duties.

"Dinah, you're so grown up, I can never quite get over it," said Ann. "You were such a mischievous mite when we first met you."

"I can imagine you as a grubby little rascal," tooted Serafina, batting her spider leg eyelashes coated in mascara.

Dinah smiled serenely. She had no hang-ups about her past childish pranks. I don't think I had ever met anyone as self-possessed as Dinah. Compared to her, Serafina was vacuous and empty-headed.

Austin and Rosemary Dill came over.

"Austin, do introduce us," said Ann.

"This is the Honourable Rosemary Dill," said Austin. "Of course, you travelled up with Ernest, Serafina, Simon, and Dinah. This is Jill Crewe, daughter of the house, Ann and Henry, our local vet in Oxfordshire."

At that moment, Frank strolled in. He had spruced himself up admirably, clean and brushed in a smart suit that looked in the American style. Again, we went on a round of introductions.

"Frank is staying up here at Blainstock. He's in the Dower House working for Yola and Jack Laskey," I explained. "But originally, he's from Chatton. He's been showjumping on the local circuit for years."

There was a chorus of good evenings and how-do-you-dos. But our circle got too big for collective conversation and broke into smaller groups. Frank and I were swept into a discussion with Austin and Rosemary on the local horse scene in Chatton. Rosemary had ridden as a child but had recently been to Switzerland, being polished up to make her debut in society. She was keen to start riding again and had been exercising Austin's chestnut gelding, Firefly, while he was supposed to be studying at Lonsdale College in Oxford.

Mummy had arranged for a rather impressive gong to be placed in the front hall, which now summoned us to partake of a buffet supper. Gertrude, Buster and Bunty were yet to arrive, also Susan and Barty. So we went in and helped ourselves to a most delicious supper that included any number of dishes. Something to suit every possible palate. First, I placed a large slice of beef and vegetable pie on my plate. Then, some delicious potato salad made with Cook's creamy mayonnaise, fresh parsley and chives from the garden, two fried chicken drumsticks coated in spices that suggested a Middle Eastern flavour, and a spoonful of rice mixed with vegetables.

"Have you noticed that we're eating food with a more international flavour?" asked Mummy, in an undertone.

"Yes, I did. It's delicious and quite adventurous for Cook," I commented.

"She's got an assistant who comes up from the village. This young woman likes experimenting with exotic flavours."

"Well, the guests certainly seem to like it," I said, as everyone helped themselves to chicken drumsticks.

I moved over to the dinner table and found myself seated next to Serafina. She was interrogating the young man called Theodore Chapman, who had come up by train with the Pevensys and Talbots. He was very attractive with light blue eyes, flaxen hair, and a becoming light tan on his skin. He had a Scandinavian look. He had spent the winter in the French Alps skiing. When he spoke, his tenor voice had a woodwind quality.

Serafina was practising her considerable arts on him, smiling coquettishly with winsomely blinking eyelids and wiggling her pretty little fingers in the air as she chatted.

Theo was faultlessly polite, talking about his winter in France with some interesting anecdotes, but he didn't seem to be responding to Serafina's charms. I decided I didn't like her at all. She was an incorrigible flirt. I felt sorry for Ernest.

Cecilia and Royce were seated at the head of the table as befitted the guests of honour. They did seem suited to each other. Sometimes, Cecilia completed Royce's sentences for him, and he would smile at her indulgently. Perhaps, it was a case of choosing a woman like one's mother. I vaguely wondered what Frank's mother was like. I had never met his parents.

I could hear Ann interrogating Dinah a few seats away.

"You and him are a proper item, then?" asked Ann, indefatigable when it came to ascertaining the nature of any new relationship.

"Whatever that means!" retorted Dinah, who had no intention of descending into the gory depths of any girlish chats about her secret feelings for Simon Caxton-Thorpe.

People were finishing their meals and drifting back to the table for second helpings. I spooned a hefty serving of apple crumble and custard into a bowl. Serafina was helping herself to a ridiculously dainty portion of fruit salad, with no cream or custard. She returned to the table and sat beside Austin. I followed her and sat opposite. I was curious about this woman who seemed determined to charm and entrance every man in the room.

I wondered if I shouldn't try a few of her techniques on Frank, but the thought of that sort of inane posturing seemed an insult to all women. Austin didn't agree. He responded with alacrity, laughing and joking, making extravagant compliments. Rosemary sat silently, sphinx-like, not betraying her feelings. She didn't seem to be a dill but a sensible young woman. She was taking Austin and Serafina's display of mutual interest very well. She turned to Ernest and engaged him in conversation, trying to restore some decent order to the dinner table relations.

Henry was on my other side, and I started chatting with him. I dangled my fingers to make a point and attempted to simper, in a clumsy imitation of Serafina.

"Is there something wrong with your hand?" asked Henry. "Are you suffering some sort of arthritic pain?"

I laughed out loud. Trust Henry to make a physiological diagnosis.

"I was practising some flirtatious gestures," I confided to him.

"I don't think they really suit you," he replied seriously as if giving advice to someone teetering on the edge of mild lunacy.

"That has put me in my place," I replied. "Obviously, I have no future as a coquette."

"I'm sure you have other life skills," he said soothingly.

At that point, Susan and Barty made an entrance. They slid over to the buffet table, perhaps embarrassed that they were arriving so late. Susan helped herself to food and marched off to sit next to Cecilia. I hadn't realised they were such good friends. Perhaps Susan was angling to be a bridesmaid, or more likely, she wanted to wedge herself into the Pevensy family as best she could. They were deep in conversation, and Barty went to the opposite end of the table and sat next to Theo, with whom he seemed to be acquainted.

I could see Susan's eyes darting towards Austin, who was becoming more and more enthusiastic about Sickening Serafina.

"Oh Mademoiselle, oh, Mademoiselle, oh, the delight of you," he said to her in a slick imitation of a French accent.

Susan looked very unhappy. I guessed that she was still holding a torch for Austin. I was surprised she hadn't seen through him, but then who was I to talk when I had been so infatuated with Jack Laskey? But that was in the dim and distant past and best forgotten.

My attention was distracted by the arrival of Buster and Gertrude. They were unmistakable in their rustic way, both with rosy complexions and shining healthy hair. Buster had a very impressive physique with shoulders at least two pickaxes across. Gertrude had matching hips, perhaps one and a half pick axes wide. A skinny girl slunk in behind them, hidden by their substantial shadows. She had extraordinary knife-edged features, piercing dark eyes and a bitter droop to her mouth. Her head hung from her scrawny neck like a snowdrop on its stalk.

Buster hailed Royce in a hearty voice, waving a paw towards him.

"Help yourself to grub," said Royce, gesturing towards the buffet table, which still had sufficient food for several more people. "Come and join us."

I could hear him introducing the newcomers to those seated around them at the top of the table. The thin girl was called Bunty Pope.

"Buster farms the land beside Pevensy Park, and Gertrude's father is a landowner in the area."

"I come from robust country stock," said Gertrude, laughing in a jolly way. Cecilia was laughing with her. She obviously felt at home with such unpretentious country people. I saw then that Cecilia was remodelling herself as a landowner's wife. It wasn't just doing good works amongst the local tenantry but enjoying the countryside with dogs and horses. I wondered if these people went out shooting. Perhaps they might be persuaded to bring up a party in August when we shot the grouse. I glanced guiltily towards Dinah, thinking she could probably divine my thoughts. I was sure that she would totally disapprove of shooting grouse.

"Look! There's a weird-looking girl over there," I waved my hand vaguely in the direction of Bunty, muttering in undertones.

"Gosh!" whispered Ann. "That nose and chin are sharp enough to cut paper."

"What are you two ratbags muttering about?" asked Henry. "Unfortunately, not everyone in the world is blessed with your own faultless features."

"Coffee will be served in the library," said Richard, standing up to address the guests.

Some declared that they were ready for bed and excused themselves. It had been a long and exhausting journey.

"Breakfast will be served at nine tomorrow morning," said Richard. "We will sound the gong at eight-thirty." He and

Mummy were very enthusiastic about this gong.

I decided that I had had enough socialising to last me for the day and tomorrow would be much more of the same. Ann agreed with me. We made our way up to my turret bedroom.

"I declare I'm going to be fast asleep the minute my head hits the pillow. No in-depth girlish chats tonight."

"Quite right," said Ann. "If we go riding together, we might be able to have a heart-to-heart along the way."

"Absolute bliss," I said sleepily as my eyelids closed.

*****

On Friday morning, the people who wanted to ride assembled in the stable yard. We were bustling around organising a mount for each person. Lavender and Morgan had saddled up and mounted Black Boy and Rex, sitting quietly chatting. We had decided to bestow a huge privilege upon Mercedes, who was given Skydancer. Frank had decided to do his duty and ride Firestorm. Cecilia was on Bonnie, who we knew would look after her, and Royce was given Balius as one of the guests of honour. Rosemary assured us she was a capable rider and was mounted on Chocolate, a former racehorse that Linda had been training. He had calmed down a lot and was no longer rushing around with his head in the air, but he wore a running martingale that restricted his head tossing behaviour. We were running short of mounts, and Susan was given Rumble, who was Linda's special project. I was on Shadow, and Ann on her favourite Copperplate.

"Hang on a minute. Where is Austin? I was sure he was over here, wanting to ride?" said Rosemary, looking around for her boyfriend, who had disappeared.

"I saw him walking along the track back to the castle," said the sharp-eyed Morgan.

"He must have changed his mind," said Linda. "We would have had to put him on Brownie." He was a good old horse, often used to carry supplies on the shooting expeditions. I doubted that Austin would have appreciated being mounted on such a worthy but uninspiring animal.

There was an impressive clatter of hoofs as we moved in a bunch out of the stable yard and up the path that led between the small stone-walled fields where the riding school ponies lifted their heads and watched us curiously. The weather was obliging, and it was sunny and promised to be clear all day.

Shadow was behaving very well. I was inordinately proud of his progress. He was becoming a pleasure to ride now that his muscles had built up and he was balanced. He had not been ridden in such a large crowd before, but all the horses were from Blainstock, and it probably suited his herd mentality to be one of a bunch.

I had sharpened up my commercial instincts, and I was calculating how much we might charge Aunt Primrose for this morning's ride. Cecilia and Royce were now counted as family, and Ann was my best friend. Frank was riding his employees' horse, and Mercedes was on Skydiver so we could charge horse hire for only Lavender, Morgan, Rosemary and Susan. I shrugged. It was better than nothing. I had now realised that making money from an equestrian enterprise was no easy feat. My opinion of Linda was already sky-high, but again I realised how well she had managed when she had run her own riding school on a shoestring.

We turned up the steep track that led through the hills and then turned north. There was a small, picturesque ruin at the end of the track. It was a good place to dismount and enjoy the view. I thought that Lavender and Morgan, and perhaps some of the more adventurous of our adult guests, might like to clamber over the old stones. The track was steep, with hillocks, dips and crags, twisting and turning. It was true trekking country with no opportunity to canter across undulating slopes.

"Jill, this is like the end of the earth. It is so wild up here," said Cecilia. "Do you miss the quiet lanes and leafy green civilisation of Oxfordshire?"

Trust Cecilia to hit upon my most secret thoughts!

"I still go down to Chatton quite a lot," I retorted sharply. I could see Frank's attention drawn by this conversation.

Ann sensed my disquiet.

"I think it is glorious! The jam and double cream on top!" she exclaimed. "So much sky, space, and the sea isn't far away."

"I think as long as you've got horses to ride, it doesn't much matter about the countryside," added Frank, coming to my rescue.

"Your facilities at Blainstock are out of this world," said Ann. "To think of all those hours, we spent schooling at the bottom of the paddock at Pool Cottage."

"I suppose you're right, and with guests at the castle, it's not like you lack social contact," said Cecilia.

"I think we should come up here in August for the shooting," said Royce. "We could put together a party and enjoy a wonderful Scottish experience. I believe some of my mother's ancestors were from Scotland. I must look it up when we get back to Pevensy Park."

Rosemary started talking to Frank, asking him about Firestorm. I heard him explaining how he worked for Yola and Jack Laskey. He pointed out Skydiver, who was easily the most elegant and impressive-looking horse in our group. I was earwigging shamelessly. I felt uneasy whenever another woman talked to Frank, and I hated myself for this reaction. Ann didn't mind when Henry chatted with other women, but they were established in their relationship. She knew where she stood. I was still in the nether world, waiting to see if something came from Frank and me.

Ann had dropped back to talk to Susan. She had got closer to our erstwhile enemy. Although perhaps school day rivalries made 'enemy' too dramatic a word. I know she felt sorry for Susan, married to the boring Barty. He wasn't much older than us, but his attitude and demeanour were like a stuffy old man. He was so uptight and respectable that I could understand how Susan had been drawn to the fun-loving, hell-raising Austin.

We reached the ruin, and Lavender and Morgan leapt down from their ponies, handed their reins to me and scampered off to clamber over the big stones. There were broken archways, a tumbledown tower and ruined walls. Brambles were growing through the cracked stones and jackdaws were nesting.

"I'm the King of the Castle, and you're the dirty rascal," sang Morgan, having reached the top of the ruined wall.

"For heaven's sake, Morgan! Come down now!" shouted Royce. "That doesn't look at all safe. How would I explain to mother if you got buried beneath a pile of rocks? Morgan laughed at him and threw her arms around wildly.

We all dismounted.

"Just ignore her, and she'll come down," said Cecilia. "I'm feeling quite stiff. I haven't ridden properly for ages."

"You're going to have to start riding again if you're going to fulfil my mother's image of everything the mistress of Pevensy Park should be," said Royce, smiling fondly at his intended.

On the way home, I suggested to Ann that we ride at the back. I felt it was time to get to exactly what Ann's future plans were. Besides, it helped distract me from my confusion about my feelings for Frank. I felt pulled in half between the lure of my old life in Chatton and the future we were trying to build at Blainstock.

"Now tell me the truth, dearest friend," I began. "I suspect that you're having second thoughts about going off to live in Bristol for the next five years."

"Oh, Jillikins! How astute you are!" cried Ann, then dropped her voice to a conspiratorial whisper. "You're absolutely right. You know how much I love our dear little village, and I know so many people and all I want to do is get married and have little Henrys and Anns."

"I think I've seen the writing on the wall for a while now," I said. "You went to Europe, going along with your mother's plans for giving you a Continental gloss, but you're a Chattonite at heart."

"I do like the idea of working with animals, but as Henry's wife. I can go around with him and be his assistant without actually getting qualified. So, do you think I'm submitting to the idea of being a little housewife?" she asked anxiously.

I didn't jump in with any quick comments. My friend's dilemma was something that needed serious deliberation.

"It's a pretty new thing, this idea that women are meant to have their own careers and not just trail along in the shadow of their husbands," I said slowly. "I don't think either of us will ever be doormats and drudges under the thumb of dominant men."

"No, you're right there," said Ann. "But having a real partnership with a man who respects you seems to be the most important thing for me these days."

"Henry is certainly a thoughtful man. I don't think he would expect you to be a subservient drudge," I replied.

"You see, originally, Henry planned to move to Bristol and work there. But now, the practice has become so big, and he is in tremendous demand. He has made quite a name for himself. If he moved, he would have to start again in the West Country."

"What does Henry think?" I asked.

"Well, he's such a decent chap. He says that if I want to get qualified in my own right, he'll support me all the way. But he suggested that he stay in Oxfordshire and I come home at weekends. I just don't think I can be bothered. If we get married, we can live at Pool Cottage and then get our own house and build a special building for the practice, a surgery to operate on cats and dogs. Henry is even talking about an operation room where we could operate on horses. You know there have been some marvellous advances in equine surgery," said Ann. "They say one day they'll be able to fix broken legs instead of just shooting the animal."

"I think you should stay in Oxfordshire," I said. "You can read books on animal practice and veterinary care, and Henry can teach you. You two would make the most marvellous team."

Ann's face cleared, like the sun coming out after a drizzly day.

"I needed to hear that," she said. "I haven't wanted to talk to Mummy and Daddy about it. But this is just the sort of advice I wanted."

"Well, that's all settled. And I expect to be the chief bridesmaid," I declared.

"Always the bridesmaid and never the bride," giggled Ann and shot me a meaningful look.

"That we are not going to talk about at this exact moment," I declared. Ann laughed out loud.

*****

I spent the afternoon cleaning tack with John. Again, I resolved to pull my weight at the stables. Somehow, I was constantly distracted and seemed to leave it to the others. Nobody said anything, but I was sure I caught Hugh's odd censorious look cast in my direction. Richard had pointed out to me that the facilities, which he owned, were in a way, my own contribution, so I didn't have to spend as much time working as the others, but it rankled.

"How did Chocolate go for that Rosemary?" asked John.

"She seemed to handle him very well. He's certainly calmed down since he was first ridden by Charles Ravenscroft in the indoor arena," I replied.

"Linda was saying that we might be able to sell him soon, just as an ordinary riding horse. He won't ever be up to much as a show prospect," said John.

"Well, I bow to any of Linda's judgements. She's the expert in buying and selling horses," I replied.

"Jack Laskey was saying the other day that they want to buy some more horses," said John.

"That would be good, more livery fees," I replied.

"They're going to Europe. They want Linda to go with them as a sort of consultant. They're offering good money," said John.

"Gosh!" I replied.

"That would mean the rest of us would have to step up," said John. "Do you think you could do the instructing for the riding school?"

"Of course, I could," I snapped. I was, after all, a qualified riding instructor. That had been the point of going on the horsemasters course at Porlock Vale. Not to mention that I had been instructing at Mrs Darcy's off and on for years.

"You're not thinking of going off again?" asked John.

It was a fair question, but it made me feel uncomfortable.

"If I'm needed here, I'll be here," I said. "I should hang around a bit more when Linda is teaching her kids. Then, I'll get to know how she likes to do things," I added. My dream of drifting down to Oxfordshire for a summer competing around the horse shows was dissolving.

"There's a few horse shows up here you could jump Balius," said John, reading my thoughts. "We could even make a day of it and take some of the students. They get to hire a pony for the whole day and go in the riding classes and the gymkhana events. I reckon they'd like that."

Privately, I had a vision of us slaving away, tightening girths, checking stirrup lengths, organising children for each of their events, and dealing with doting parents demanding that their children win a rosette. I realised just how spoiled I'd been: going off showjumping in Australia, studying at Porlock Vale, and before that, going to Germany to do dressage. I was going to have to knuckle down and do some honest toil, and it looked like this summer would be a time of reckoning.

"I'll have to talk to Linda and Hugh about it," I said.

"Why don't we have a Blainstock Stables meeting soon?" suggested John.

"Good idea," I agreed.

Frank came in carrying Skydiver's dressage saddle and bridle. He set to stripping the saddle and soaping it down carefully. The three of us worked companionably together.

*****

Dinner that night was formal. I slipped into a dress of crêpe de Chine, a poem in dark blue, with a sweetheart neckline and a fitted bodice. It made me look very grown up. Twirling in front of the mirror, I realised Frank had never seen me dressed up. Perhaps it would inspire him to step up and declare his undying love. Although, he certainly didn't look at me with sheep's eyes like Ernest when he was gazing at Serafina. I gave myself a mental shake. I wouldn't want a man to look at me like that. I wanted a partnership, not to be put on a pedestal.

Aunt Primrose had done the seating plan. I found myself with Frank on my left. On my right was Austin. Opposite us was Serafina, Henry, and Susan. Aunt Primrose had no idea of Susan's former clandestine relationship with Austin, or she would never have seated them opposite each other. Barty was down the table, seated between Ann and Aggie. It was going to be an entertaining meal. With Frank beside me, looking almost unrecognisable in black tie getup, Serafina the insufferable flirt, and Susan smouldering away at Austin, I might find it hard to concentrate on my food.

Inadvertently, I put the cat amongst the pigeons with my first conversational sally.

"I thought you were riding with us this morning, Austin, and then you disappeared. What did you get up to this morning?"

Susan shot me a venomous look. Serafina simpered, and Austin looked at me as if I had asked a trick question. I was about to put my first spoonful of vichyssoise into my mouth, and stopped, my spoon suspended.

"Austin very kindly took me on a tour of the gardens. You do have a most wonderful rose arbour here," said Serafina in a tinkling fairy voice.

The first thought that struck me, which fortunately I didn't say out loud, was how on earth Austin had any knowledge of the layout of our gardens as he had never been here before.

"We had a gardener who was very keen on roses, and Mummy has been tending them," I commented lamely. "I'm particularly fond of the ones that are a mixture of yellow and orange. Like little sunrises."

"We had a good ride this morning," said Frank, manfully rising to the occasion. "How did you find Rumble, Susan? Linda has been training him for a few weeks now and thinks he is very promising."

"He was a good ride," said Susan. "Can he jump?"

"Yes, he's got quite a pop in him. Linda had thought he might be an eventer, but perhaps he would do well as a steeplechaser," replied Frank.

"Jill and I had a bash at steeplechasing," said Susan, "we were neck and neck in the ladies' race at Grassmere."

You were riding that devilish black horse, appropriately named Diablo," I reminisced.

"You ended up hanging around your horse's neck across the finish line. He was a battered old thing," said Susan waspishly.

"But we won!" I pointed out.

"Gosh! That would have been worth seeing," said Austin.

"Porsche was there that day. She was competing on Rapide. It was the first time I met someone in your family," I suddenly remembered.

"Now, Porsche is the proud owner of Diablo," added Susan. "Remember we swapped, and I have the darling Sassy Swoop." She looked meaningfully at Austin, probably willing him to remember when they had met in the first flush of their illicit dalliance.

"I don't like horses at all," tooted Serafina. "They're so big and awkward. I always think they're going to tread on me."

We stared at her. We might not have all been best friends, but the five of us were deeply committed to horses in some way or another. She was obviously blissfully unaware of her *faux pas*.

I regarded her with unbridled horror as if she were an alien who had just dropped to earth. She giggled as if she had said something vastly amusing.

You would have thought that Austin would lose all interest in her at that point. Somehow it seemed to egg him on to further efforts, or possibly he was making it entirely plain to Susan that he considered himself a free agent. He was inconstancy personified, shredding women with his heartless dalliances. But, perhaps, in Serafina, he might have met his match.

"Does your husband ride?" he asked Susan pointedly.

"You know perfectly well he doesn't," she retorted, then looked like she was going to burst into tears.

At this point, I felt sorry for her. I could see why Austin had entranced her, but now he was taunting her. First, he turned up with Rosemary, flirted outrageously with Serafina, and then pointed out to Susan that she was married to a man who didn't even ride horses. A clear demonstration of heartless cruelty. I didn't know where to take the conversation. But then, Frank showed me just what a wonderful man he was.

"Serafina, I believe that Ernest has written a volume of poetry about you and your fair beauty," he said. I don't know how he had come upon this nugget of knowledge, but it certainly did the trick. Serafina began to wax lyrical about the lovely verses that the poor, deluded Ernest had composed as an eloquent tribute to her feminine perfection. At the same time, Henry turned to Susan and talked to her about Sassy Swoop and her plans to ride her in hack classes that summer. It was up to me to engage Austin in some diverting dialogue, but I couldn't think of a thing I wanted to say to him. As far as I was concerned, he was a pitiful specimen of humanity, and I hoped that the estimable Rosemary would have his measure and dump him.

The first course was over, and the staff came around and took our plates away. Richard rose to his feet, tapped his knife against a glass and announced that all the men should stand and move four seats to their left. I sighed in relief. Anything to get Austin away from Susan. He was continuing to needle her with the fact that he had no further interest in her. She might not be a perfect person but she certainly didn't deserve that.

For the main course, I now had Royce on my left, Ernest the hapless poet on my right, and opposite was Chumley. The rigours of making social conversation had exhausted me, and I thought I might retire for the night, claiming to suffer from a migraine. Tackling a difficult cross-country course, or even breaking in a bronco, had to be easier than this sort of activity. I turned my attention to the delicious salmon served with several spoonfuls of creamy pasta and topped with asparagus spears. Royce was a delight, and I thought how lucky Cecilia was to have caught herself such a husband. He seemed to know exactly what to say to everyone. His social poise was outstanding. Perhaps he might have been a diplomat in Foreign Affairs rather than a landowner tending to stock and fields all day.

"What did you do this morning, Chumly?" I asked.

"Canoeing. Great fun. Fantastic exercise," he replied in staccato phrases.

"Really!" I said. "Have you got your costume for tomorrow night sorted out?"

"By Jove, yes. Got my old scout uniform. Sort of military look," he confided proudly.

"Have you got many badges?" asked Susan. Something I had never known about her, she had been an enthusiastic girl guide.

I melted with gratitude that these two had something in common and concentrated on my food as they exchanged notes about their years of scouting and guiding.

"Ernest, I believe you're a prolific writer of verse," I said bravely, conscious that this man was utterly infatuated with the little minx, Serafina.

He put down his knife and fork and, looking across the table, began to recite. It was all I could do not to burst into uncontrollable giggles. Serafina was sitting there, entirely unembarrassed, perfect little dimples impressed on her flawless cheeks. I looked down at the table, and Ann was watching. She raised her eyebrows at me, and I snorted in a most unladylike manner. I grabbed my napkin and clasped it to my face in an effort to suppress any other sound effects.

I shovelled in the salmon. It fell apart on the fork, the most succulent fish I had ever eaten. However, in such company it was hard to concentrate on the food, which as you know is very important to me.

I was dreading Richard announcing that men jump back onto the merry-go-round, and I would find myself with a new set of conversational puzzles. Mummy had been surveying the dinner party, and she whispered something in Richard's ear. I hoped she had suggested that everything was right as it was.

Before dessert was served, Uncle Henry heaved himself to his feet. He waited for silence and made a long-winded and serious speech about the importance of marriage and how pleased he was that his Cecilia was embarking upon the marital path with such an estimable young man who would cherish her all her life. I was squirming and noticed several of our guests sitting with serious expressions. I waited for Austin to pipe up with a sarcastic comment, but he kept silent.

Uncle Henry burbled on. I had never known him to be prone to such verbosity. Eventually, Aggie leapt to her feet and thanked him profusely. She told everyone how happy they would be to welcome Cecilia to the family and proposed a toast. The table of guests enthusiastically lifted their glasses and chanted, 'to Cecilia and Royce', and gulped down the champagne that the Pevensys had thoughtfully brought up with them. I decided that if I ever did get engaged, I would never put myself through this type of painful charade.

Dessert was something different, meringue, baked crispy on the outside, soft and marshmallowy on the inside, with fresh fruit and cream. The exotic tropical fruits such as mango and guava must be brought up from Harrods. Nothing like that was available in Kilkarny or probably even Aberdeen. Every mouthful was a sensory experience of heaven. I gulped down more champagne and drifted into a waking dream where I was lying under the shade of a coconut tree somewhere in the Caribbean. I was not prone to drinking alcohol. Usually, I didn't like the woozy feeling, but tonight I began to understand the state of altered consciousness that drove people to the bottle. Anything but the grinding reality of a group of ill-assorted people crisscrossed with problematic emotions and relationships.

Finally, the torturous dinner was over, and people were drifting upstairs to the library for coffee and chocolates. As the daughter of the house, I could not just stump off to bed, so I went with the crowd. At least I could choose who to sit near and chat with. I was gratified that Frank plonked himself down beside me. Sometimes I wondered if I had totally imagined that there was something more than friendship between us. He was certainly playing his cards close to his chest.

"You know you scrub up well," he said to me with a cheeky grin. This must be his version of a compliment.

"Thank you, kind sir," I replied. I had read that somewhere in a book.

"Oh, Frank and Jill," said Ann, snuggling down between us on the sofa. I looked at her, wondering if she were doing this deliberately. "Are we riding to the sea tomorrow?"

"That's the plan," I said.

"Oh, goodie! And can I have Copperplate again? She is an absolute darling."

"Of course," I said. "Which horse will you ride, Frank, assuming you're coming?"

"Definitely. I haven't done this famous ride to the sea yet, and it might even be warm enough to paddle in the water. I think I'll have to ride Firestorm again. Jack wants him fit, and it will be a good day's work for him. The problem is that the fitter he gets, the more boisterous."

"What about me?" asked Henry. "Which horse do I get?"

"Well, you went sailing with Richard today? How did that go?" I asked.

"Fabulous, nothing like skimming across the top of all those little waves," said Henry.

"Susan rode Rumble today. He's a thoroughbred that Linda is training. Hopefully, she won't mind you riding him tomorrow. He's going well."

"That's me sorted then," said Henry.

"I suppose I'll ride Shadow again. I certainly don't want any of the guests messing him up. He's coming on nicely."

"I don't think Skydancer should go all that way, just in case something happens to him. I mean Mercedes handled him very well today, but Lola didn't really give permission for him to be ridden by other people," said Frank.

"Imagine if he twisted a tendon. That's £20,000 worth of broken-down horse," I commented.

"Exactly," said Frank.

*****

Austin, Rosemary, Serafina and Ernest were destined to sail together on the following day. Apparently, Rosemary was an experienced sailor, and she would be able to handle the boat as Richard had to drive down to the coast with our picnic.

"That's going to be an interesting combination," I muttered to Ann. "It's a tossup whether Rosemary will drown Serafina or Ernest will make sure that Austin gets knocked out by the boom."

"Gosh!" said Ann. "I'm glad that Henry isn't like that. He's such a steady, decent chap. I know that I can always rely on him."

"You've got a model relationship," I replied. Ann gave me a look but did not comment.

The undercurrents were swirling beneath us like a combination of rip tides going to sweep us all to disaster.

*****

"It's going to be a long ride and then the fancy dress dance tonight," said Mummy. "Do you think you're up to it?"

"I'm young and fit," I said. "You haven't told me what I'm meant to be wearing tonight?"

"Ha ha!" said Mummy, triumphantly as if she had scored a victory. "I'll bring it up to your room tonight when you're ready to dress. You're going to adore it!"

This boded no good at all. Perhaps it was a Little Miss Muffit outfit or even worse, Humpty Dumpty.

I went down to the stables early. There were eleven of us riding to the sea, and Linda would be busy with her Saturday morning riding school kids. I saddled up Bonnie for Gertrude, Balius for Mercedes, Brownie for Buster, Turpin for Theo and Cammie for Bunty. Lavender and Morgan were fussing over Black Boy and Rex, and Ann and Henry were saddling Rumble and Copperplate. Three of the most competent riding school students, Kirsty, Ellie and Maddie, had been booked to come with us, but Linda had suggested that they not go. Instead, they could spend the day with her riding in her lessons on different horses. She would make sure they had an interesting day.

The weather was closing in, and I thought such a long ride was a risk, but we didn't want to deviate from our schedule. I zipped back to the castle and suggested to Richard that he bring some macks with the lunch. Mummy took me aside and persuaded me that such a long ride with bad weather threatening was not a good idea. Black clouds were massing across the tops of the mountains. A cold breeze was rushing down towards us.

In the stable yard, the horses were restless, tossing their heads.

"I'm not sure that going such a long way is going to be possible," said Henry.

"Henry don't be such a killjoy! We're robust enough to withstand a little rain," objected Ann.

"A Highland storm can be violent," I said, looking at the ominous clouds. The gusting wind brought down the sound of deep rumbling. "I think we're going to have to call it off."

"Why don't we go for a quick canter around the loch and see what the weather does?" suggested Ann.

Off we set. Black Boy and Rex led the way, ridden by young Lavender and Morgan. Black Boy's steady canter was the same speed as little Rex's amazingly quick trot. Ann and Henry were hot on their heels. Rumble was obviously harking back to his racing days and was cantering sideways, trying to take the lead. Copperplate was her usual perfect self, cantering sedately at the exact pace set by her rider. Mercedes followed in their wake on Balius. I couldn't help but admire my promising horse. His head was bent correctly at the poll, and he carried his hindquarters beneath him. He and Mercedes made a very attractive picture.

"Good boy," said Mercedes, stroking him softly on his neck. "What a good horse you are."

Buster, Gertrude and Bunty rode in a bunch, three abreast, trotting quietly. Bunty was obviously a novice, mounted on Cammie, who was a very quiet riding school pony.

"Hold onto the pommel, dear. Up, down, up, down. That's good. You're getting the rhythm of it," said Gertrude. She demonstrated a maternal attitude towards Bunty.

"I've got it!" said Bunty breathlessly.

Theo was riding behind them. He was mounted on Turpin, another of the quiet riding school horses.

"Well done! Bunty!" he called encouragingly.

Bunty continued to lurch up and down.

Frank and I brought up the rear. Firestorm was walking out well. Somehow, Frank had persuaded himself to proceed calmly. He seemed to have a magic touch with difficult horses.

"Come on, let's trot. We must keep up with the others," I said.

The wind was whistling. Sweeping down from the mountains, the stormy air swirled around us.

"Look, that sailing boat is whizzing along!" called Gertrude. "This wind really fills out the sails."

Then the rain came. Pelting, freezing icy rain, slanting across the air into our faces.

"We must ride for home!" I called, spinning Shadow on his hocks, forgetting for a moment that he was a novice horse who had to be ridden carefully.

We clattered back to the stable yard. Each of us pulled the saddles off and shunted the horses into their stables. I handed out old towels which were piled high in the tack room cupboard for such occasions, and we set to with gusto, rubbing down the damp horses. Each of them was then swaddled in a warm stable blanket and given a full hay net.

The group crowded into the tack room, and I put fresh wood into the stove that was kept burning most days, for making tea, bran mashes and sometimes even a wholesome stew with dumplings which Linda made for the workers to have a hot lunch without having to go back to the cottage or John's rooms in the castle.

"This is absolutely spliffikins! Such a cosy room!" enthused Ann, setting out mugs for tea. "You've got such a wonderful set-up here, Jill."

"I know. Not something I ever dreamed of back in Pool Cottage. Not that two loose boxes, a small paddock and an orchard were anything to be sniffed at."

"Perhaps you could adopt me?" suggested Lavender in a small voice. "Black Boy is still my heart horse. I mean Summer Fancy is beautiful, and everything a dream show pony should be, but it isn't the same as one's first love."

I knew that she was also thinking about her uncomfortable home life with the spiky hot house flowers and the abrasive demeanour of her mother.

"You can come and stay in the holidays if you like," I suggested. "All three of you. I think Ruby would like it up here."

"She's having to look after her mother at the moment," said Morgan. "She got pneumonia in the winter and still isn't right."

I knew Ruby lived in a drab caravan in a horrible muddy yard strewn with rubbish. They pinched and scrimped and starved and only just got by. I wondered what might happen to her if her mother died. Her father came and went as it suited him. I doubted if he would take on the full-time care of the lively, spirited Ruby. Perhaps the Pevensys would take her in, as they had taken in Mark Lansdowne. Or Mrs Whirtley, who had so kindly tucked Dinah Dean under her wing.

The rain lightened, and we made a dash back to the castle for lunch. Mummy had set out the picnic items, supplemented with cold meat pies, hot leek and potato soup, and fresh crusty bread. After we had eaten, most of the people went into the games room. A darts match was proposed, and two teams were arranged. I was hopeless at darts. They would never stick into the board and fell fatally to the floor. Occasionally, they did stick but only when they missed the board entirely and went into the wall. I went out to the kitchen and helped Cook with clearing away and preparing the buffet supper that would be served tonight.

Then, Mummy came in and suggested that we go up to my room, and I could try on the outfit that she had organised for me tonight. She was brimming with excitement, her eyes aglow. She told me that she had arranged a similar outfit for herself. I was still a little nervous that it might be a nursery rhyme character or something equally childish or comic.

I gasped in surprise when I saw it laid out on my bed. It was the most divine ball dress. A proper Cinderella outfit that would be suitable for a royal occasion. Beautiful turquoise silk with a closely fitted sleeveless bodice and skirt that flared extravagantly from the waist and fell in perfect folds to the ground.

"I love this colour!" I gasped.

"You don't think it's too much?" asked Mummy anxiously.

"No, it is perfect. As bright as a peacock."

"And here is a darling little stole," she said, wrapping something white and furry around my shoulders. "And dainty white dancing shoes."

"But how is it fancy dress?" I asked.

"I have this Italian masque, hand-made, from Venice. You hold it up with this wooden rod. We can do your hair up in a fancy style, and you'll be the belle of the ball."

"I don't want to eclipse Cecilia," I said.

"Nonsense, it's each woman for herself when it comes to dressing up," said Mummy. "No longer are you going to hide yourself under a bushel. Seriously, Jill, it's time for you to get out there. Let it be your time to shine."

"What are you wearing?" I asked, desperate to change the topic.

"The same style in a soft-rose colour. I can't carry off bright colours at my age," replied Mummy. "I got Kitty to make them." She was the dressmaker in the village.

Ann came in as I was twirling in front of the mirror.

"Oh, Jill! You look scrumptious. You'll have every man in the room falling at your feet," she exclaimed.

"Well, at least one, as long as it is the right one," said Mummy meaningfully. I blushed like a beetroot.

"What are you wearing, Ann?" I asked, changing the subject.

"Henry and I have matching harlequin outfits. We've got some golden balls to juggle and some hoops decorated with bright ribbons. We're to be court jesters."

"That sounds fun," I said. "Where did you get costumes like that?"

"There's a shop in Rychester that rents out outfits. Fancy dress has become all the thing."

Ann opened her suitcase and produced her outfit.

"Well, put it on and see how it looks," I urged.

Mummy went off to her room to get dressed. I sat in front of the dressing table and began applying my makeup.

"I'll do it for you," volunteered Ann. She brushed on blusher copiously and then scrubbed it off with a handkerchief.

"What is the point of putting it on and rubbing it off?" I asked peevishly.

"It's meant to produce a more *naturel* effect."

I scowled into the mirror.

"If the wind changes, your face will stay like that," scolded Ann.

"You sound like a great-aunt," I snapped. Mummy and Ann were obviously in cahoots over this project to polish up my appearance.

Eventually, we were ready and after a last prance in front of the mirror we descended to help Mummy with the last minute arrangements.

The band from Edinburgh were tuning up in the banqueting hall. The long tables and chairs had been pushed back against the wall to make room for dancing. A woman from the village was pushing around a polishing rag on the end of a mop. Cecilia was perched on a step-ladder hanging streamers along the walls, looping them around picture hooks and stringing them up across the ceiling.

"Jill and Ann! Can you take over!" she called. "I want to go and get dressed."

We could hear shrieks and scuffles coming down the stairs. Various guests flashed around, some recognisable and others not. I was keeping a sharp eye out for Frank, who had refused to divulge his outfit. However, I was momentarily distracted as I caught a glimpse of a glamorous Marilyn

Monroe entering the room. It took me a minute to identify Susan King. She was wearing an extravagant blonde wig, bright red lipstick, and a copy of that iconic white dress that had billowed upwards when the real Marilyn had stood over an upward draft from a grill in the pavement.

"My goodness!" I exclaimed.

"Jumping Russian rabbits," gasped Ann, echoing my astonishment.

"She looks splendid!" I said. I would never have dared to make such a public display of my charms, such as they were. Our Susan was evolving into a dramatic creature. "If that doesn't turn Austin's head, then nothing will!"

"Absolutely!" said Ann. "I think I shall have to keep a keen eye on Henry."

"I don't think you've got much to worry about there," I said soothingly, suddenly worrying that Frank might have a secret thing about Marilyn Monroe.

"Oh, look!" said Ann, laughing merrily. "As the bishop said to the actress."

Barty King entered dressed as a clergyman.

"They will have to win first prize," I announced.

"Are there prizes?" asked Ann.

"Not that I know of."

"Sickening Serafina is going to find it hard to eclipse such a sexy Marilyn Monroe," I muttered under my breath.

"She's certainly making an effort," said Ann, nodding towards the doorway.

Serafina knew how to make an entrance. She was wearing a filmy layered dress in the colours of apple blossom. Although she was undoubtedly beautiful, she was preening like a jackdaw in peacock feathers, spoiling the woodland nymph look. But, perhaps, I was being too critical. Personally, I would have rather painted my toenails with poison than display my body in such a brazen fashion.

"I think you've forgotten your skirt," said Rosemary pointedly, in a loud carrying voice that could be heard all over the room.

Serafina shot her a searing look of malice. Rosemary smiled benignly.

"What an array of beautiful young women we have tonight!" said Mummy cheerfully, coming to help us with our overhead streamers. "Such a variety of beauty."

"You're holding your own," said Richard gallantly. He was dressed in his kilt. I had to agree; Mummy did look glamorous in her shimmering rose-pink gown, a vision of mature elegance.

"A photographer is coming up from London to take pictures," said Mummy. "Aggie has just told me. It's that Hetty, who was here undercover during the filming of *Macbeth*. It is going to be the most marvellous publicity for the castle. We'll have a record of all of you in your dazzling costumes twirling on the ballroom floor. I think we might even be able to break into the wedding market. Can you imagine Jill? High society weddings can be very costly!"

"More shekels in the coffers," I agreed enthusiastically. "But the last time I saw Hetty, she was a sub-editor, aiming for editor. Why would she be freelancing as a photographer for private events."

"I have no idea," said Mummy absent-mindedly.

"Oh, look!" exclaimed Ann, again pointing towards the door.

It was a pantomime version of Black Boy, prancing in across the floor. He was bowing to his admirers, who were laughing and clapping.

"It must be Lavender and Morgan," I said. "They've had a costume made especially like Black Boy!"

A moment after the entrance of the pantomime horse, Hetty arrived, carrying an extremely impressive camera with knobs and twiddly bits and attachments.

"Good evening, Jill," she said as I was standing near the door. "No time, long see. How's the writing going?"

"Not bad, but lots of distractions. Mummy said you were coming up to take photos. I thought you were a sub-editor now?"

"That's right. This is just a one-off, a bit of pocket money. Aggie is paying my expenses and the cost of the photos, and I get to write up the event for various magazines. Hopefully, you'll all be gracing the social pages."

"Good-oh," I said, "all great publicity. By the way, here is the engaged couple now. If you want to get clicking."

Cecilia and Royce's entrance was somewhat disappointing. Amongst the elegant women already assembled, Cecilia looked over-dressed and clumsy. Her face was painted white with round circles of rouge on her cheekbones and too many beauty spots dotted around her mouth. Her dress was fussy, with far too many swirls of embroidery, sequins, silver tubes, buttons and bows. It was a bit of a damp squib.

In contrast, Mercedes swanned in a few moments later. She was dressed in a Japanese costume, whitened face, red lips, mask-like face, mysterious and unbearably exotic, walking with tiny steps like a perfect geisha. She made such an entrance that there was a moment of silence. Serafina, looking underdressed, wasn't happy.

The lady with the mop had disappeared. Richard carried away the step ladder. The band struck up the first number. The lights were dimmed, and the night's ceremony was to begin. Some women from the village, dressed in smart black and white uniforms, were circulating with trays of champagne glasses. A footman dressed in tails carried another tray of glasses with scotch for the men who preferred a more serious drink.

"Jill and Ann, would you mind circulating with these *hors d'oeuvres*," said Mummy.

It gave us a chance to listen in to snippets of conversation passing between the guests. Frank had still not made an appearance. I wondered if he might have decided not to come. At such a thought, the backs of my knees ached in a mixture of disappointment and unhappiness, like going down in a lift meant to be going up.

"What's up, Jillikins?" asked Ann. "You look stricken."

"Nothing. Nothing at all," I replied, pulling myself together.

Hastily, I offered my tray of delicacies to Dinah, Simon and Austin. Dinah was dressed as a committed Chinese Communist, with a snugly tailored Mao suit and a pair of black cloth shoes. Her crowning feature was a cap with a small peak and red star sewn on the front. Simon was dressed in a blue Chinese military suit with red panels sewn on the collar and a blue cap with a red star. Austin was Robin Hood, which matched Rosemary's Maid Marion outfit.

"We have to fight communism," said Austin, who had adopted an authoritarian and unusually serious voice. "If we don't, we shall lose our freedom, not to mention our inherited birth right."

"By that, you mean unearned inherited privilege based on the fact that the aristocracy somehow thinks they're inherently superior to the common herd. It's that old myth that the blood of the gods is mixed with mortals," retorted Dinah. "There are different types of communism. The Chinese are

the good guys, not like the Russians with their gulags and the KGB. The credibility of the US government is at an all-time low with young intellectuals of our generation."

"That's not very patriotic. We should be proud to be British. We do things correctly in Britain," said Austin. I was surprised that he seemed so serious, not his usual flippant, disrespectful style.

"You're nothing but a jumped-up guttersnipe," hissed Serafina at Dinah, taking the argument to the worst level of personal insults. I gasped. What Serafina had said was beyond the pale. Simon might have biffed her on the nose if she had been a man, but he was too much of a gentleman to attack a female.

At that point, Hetty materialised beside me.

"Come on, bunch up. Smile. Now I need your names, your occupation, if you have one and not just a trust fund, and where you live."

"You know me," said Austin.

"Of course, you're Rosemary's boyfriend," said Hetty.

"Dinah Dean, law student at Cambridge, and this is my boyfriend," Dinah said with a note of pride in her voice, "Simon Caxton-Thorpe, he's from Birtle, Oxfordshire, and he's a poet."

"Serafina Collins," simpered the other member of the group. "I live in Oxford. My father is the vicar at St Augustine's."

"A vicar's daughter!" said Hetty with a wry twist of her lips.

"Serafina, I wondered if you might help us hand around some of these savouries," I suggested, desperate to get her away from Dinah before a full-scale brawl broke out. I thrust the tray upon her and putting my hand in the small of her back, propelled her several yards away to a group made up of Gertrude, Buster, Bunty, Chumley and Rosemary. She looked mulish. Being a glorified waitress was the last thing she wanted to do, but she could hardly refuse, without dumping the tray and physically warding off my determined guiding arm.

Gertrude was dressed as Snow White and Buster as an evil witch. They looked like they would do well in a pantomime. I was impressed with the creativity of their costumes, especially Buster, with an impressive carbuncle on the end of his false nose. Bunty was dressed as Little Bo Peep. Her prominent chin and slitty black eyes were entirely at odds with her cutesy outfit, complete with a wig of golden ringlets and a crook which was decorated with ribbons like a maypole.

Finally, Frank came sliding through the door, wearing a scarecrow outfit. I have to admit that I was disappointed. He looked like an unmade bed. Most of us had attempted to enhance our appearance with an outfit that made us more glamorous and beautiful. A scarecrow! What was the significance of that? Perhaps there was a deeper meaning that I had to fathom.

Cecilia swanned up to Frank and pulled him over towards me. This was even more disconcerting.

"You must dance with Jill!" she announced loudly and commandingly.

"Certainly," said Frank obediently.

I stood with my mouth open like a goldfish.

"What's your game?" I muttered to Cecilia.

"Oh, Jill! I've just decided you and Frank are a perfect couple, and I'm determined to matchmake you," announced Cecilia.

This had to be the most devastating and tactless comment ever uttered by my meddlesome cousin. I knew from long experience that once Cecilia seized upon an idea, she stayed seized, and there was nothing I could do about it.

Frank held out his hand, and I took it, and we proceeded to the area of the floor, which was for dancing. The band was playing a merry waltz, and Frank put his arm around me, his hand firmly in the small of my back. I put one hand on his shoulder and the other hand in his. We three-stepped around the floor.

"Don't worry about what Cecilia says," he told me. "I'm my own man, I would have asked you to dance anyway."

I was utterly mortified. I wanted to slide down onto the floor and between the cracks in the floorboards. Secretly, I might have longed to be in Frank's arms in a romantic clinch, but now it was dust and ashes. I never wanted to talk to him again. The dance finished, and I excused myself and rushed from the room, leaping up the stairs until I reached my turret bedroom. Hot tears were welling in my eyes.

I felt like I would never descend the stairs again. Then, Mummy tapped on my door.

"Jill, can I come in?"

She sat on the edge of my bed. "I know what Cecilia said. She told me. She was trying to help you, but it was entirely tactless. I'm so sorry. Cecilia will never say another word, she has promised."

"I can't face him! Not after this! It is just too humiliating!"

"Now Jill, you mustn't exaggerate. It's not that bad. It was a stupid, tactless comment. If you weren't very fond of Frank, then you would have laughed it off without a second thought. In the grand scheme of things, it's not the end of the world."

I snuffled into my pillow. I was determined to play the Tragedy Queen. This was the end of all my romantic dreams. Mummy sat there, gently stroking my hair.

"We really need to go down and attend to the guests. You never know. This might help to resolve the situation between you and Frank. He will either come to the point, or he will withdraw."

"Ohh," I groaned. "I could kill Cecilia."

"I know, but truly she meant well. Come downstairs. Don't even think about it. Try and enjoy yourself."

"The chances of that are zilch," I said melodramatically.

"The more upset you look, the worse it will be. Carry your head high and act like you don't care," advised Mummy. "Come on."

I followed her downstairs.

*****

The band was having a break and most of the guests were in the dining room helping themselves to supper from the buffet table. After everyone had eaten there was another toast to the happy couple. Then, the band struck up again.

Richard insisted that I dance with him. He tried to teach me the jitter bug and I couldn't help but collapse with giggles at my inept attempts. I dared not look around the room in case my eye caught Frank's. After Richard led me off the floor, Theo fetched up by my side, wearing a dragon's outfit. He was clad in a close-fitting green scaly body suit with a long tail swishing behind him and a dragon head hat that could be pulled over his face or be pushed up like a tall hat if he wanted to talk, eat or drink. He led me onto the floor, and we did a version of a rock and roll dance. I forgot my chagrin at Cecilia's remark. Two glasses of white wine and the amusing antics of Theo, who was probably the most handsome man in the room, certainly helped. Ann and Henry came and danced beside us. The pantomime Black Boy clomped around us in a circle in a funny sort of rolling step. Next, Aggie and Louis came onto the dance floor and showed their spirited side, doing a sort of rockabilly dance. Aggie was dressed as an angel, and Louis as a demon. We all laughed ourselves silly. Then, Frank and Bunty were dancing as well. They looked ridiculous, a rustic scarecrow and Little Bo Peep. I was light-headed and tipsy and suddenly my earlier burst of despair seemed ridiculously over the top.

There was a slow dance at the end of the night and Frank came up to me and led me onto the floor.

"Cecilia was right. We do make a good couple," he murmured in my ear. "What do you think?"

I nodded my head. I couldn't find any words.

"We'll talk about it in a few days when everybody leaves. In private."

Again, I nodded my head. I was happy that he was being masterful. Just the way I thought a man should behave.

*****

We all slept in on Sunday morning. At half past nine, churchgoers were summoned by Mummy and Richard's gong. Surprisingly, I had not tossed and turned all night but slept well. Ann and I were so exhausted that when we went to bed, there had been no time for girlish confidences. I had wanted to hug my happiness about Frank to myself. It was too precious to share yet. I was sure that Ann would cotton on soon enough, with her sharp eyes and lively sense of curiosity.

The six sets of parents were drinking tea and eating toast dressed in sober church-going outfits. I joined them for breakfast but was determined to head over to the stables to do my bit. There would be riding school students today, and I wanted to show willing. Mercedes was sitting at the table, obviously planning to go to church. She was such a well-behaved young woman that she must have a good effect on Mark Lansdowne. Cecilia and Royce joined the group. Dinah and Ernest wandered in.

"Are you two joining us for the morning service?" asked Mummy

Dinah said, "I do not care to attend the shop-worn conventions of an outmoded religion. Nor am I interested in any stream-of-consciousness narratives from a preacher who claims to be in close connection to a deity."

Ernest gaped at her, probably thinking it was early in the morning for such higher-level abstract thinking.

"Serafina is sure to go to church. Her father is a vicar, isn't he?" said Mercedes, skipping over any discomfort caused by Dinah's pronouncement.

"Where is Serafina? She's lazing in bed no doubt. She hasn't come down to breakfast," said Cecilia. I noticed an edge to my cousin's voice. She knew that Royce had been momentarily infatuated with the divinely dainty

Serafina when he had first met her. I think she was keeping an eye on the simpering miss.

"I'll go up and take her a cup of tea. We don't want her missing church." I suggested, thinking it would serve her right to be hauled from bed and sent to the morning service.

She certainly needed some spiritual guidance when it came to the way that she treated other people.

"She's in the blue room," said Mummy.

I stumped up the stairs and knocked on the painted-blue door, but there was no reply. I opened the door and saw that the bed had not been slept in. I thought that she might have sneaked in with Austin.

"I don't think she's planning to go to church this morning," I said, prevaricating as best I could when I returned to the dining room.

Ernest was now committed to attending church and went off with the others. I imagined he had only made an effort to impress Serafina. My dislike of that young woman intensified. She was most definitely a hussy!

Other guests began to drift down to the dining room. I went to the kitchen, fetched more toast and a coffee pot, and then hurried over to the stables. All the loose boxes had been mucked out, so I helped with grooming the ponies and tacking up for the next lesson. Linda was already in the indoor arena with six students.

"How did last night go?" asked John.

"It was fun. We danced into the night. Everyone made an effort with the dressing up."

"Frank said he was going as a scarecrow," said John.

"Yes, that's right." My face had gone bright red with embarrassment. I thrust my head under Oriole's saddle flap, ostensibly to check the girth, to hide my confusion. The next lot of pupils were arriving, and John went into the office to deal with the payments and parents' enquiries.

Lavender and Morgan turned up.

"We thought we might head off for a ride by ourselves," said Lavender. "If that's alright with you, Jill?"

"I'm sure that is fine. Even if you lose your way, the ponies will be able to find their way back."

I helped the next round of children to mount, checking stirrup lengths and tightening girths. The riders who had finished their lesson came back from the arena, and I supervised the dismounting. We loosened girths and put headcollars on over the bridles so that the ponies could be hitched to the centre rail, ready for lessons later in the day. I went around with a bucket offering each of them a drink. I noticed that Misty's tail was knotted, and I fetched a body brush to smooth it out. The routine riding school activity gave me time to think about the previous night's events. Frank and I were going to talk about our relationship. I knew that it was time that we sorted it, but at the same time, I was dreading it.

By lunchtime, I was more than ready for sustenance. I hurried back to the castle to see what was on the menu. The churchgoers were back from the morning service at Craigie. Mummy, Aunt Primrose and Aggie were supervising a big cleanup of the banqueting hall. Some of the guests were sitting out in the garden sipping coffee and chatting. Others were up in the library, ensconced in armchairs, reading the morning newspapers.

Sunday lunch was traditional roast beef with Yorkshire pudding and Cook's special roast potatoes done with lashings of dripping. I was poised over my plate with knife and fork in hand, ready to do justice to such a magnificent meal, when Ernest announced that Serafina was missing.

"Where is Serafina?" he cried in tones of distress. He looked anxious and upset. I didn't want to say that her bed hadn't been slept in. Everybody looked around as if expecting her to be tucked into a corner and out of sight.

"Jill, you went to look for her this morning?" said Mummy quietly.

"Her bed hadn't been slept in," I whispered back. Mummy frowned.

"Come on, let's go and look," she said quietly.

I motioned to Ann, and the three of us went upstairs and searched each of the guest rooms. She was not in any of the beds. We even looked into the wardrobes. Ann and I were treating it as a bit of a joke.

"The library," said Mummy. "Perhaps she fell asleep in a chair and has been overlooked."

We searched methodically, but no Serafina could be found.

"This is rather disturbing," said Mummy. "Thankfully, Hetty has set off for London. It wouldn't do the castle much good if it were known that we were losing guests."

"Could she have hitched a lift with Hetty and left without saying anything?" asked Ann.

"No, I went out to the car with Hetty and waved her off," replied Mummy. "Unless Serafina waylaid her along the road outside the castle gates and got in then."

"What reason could she possibly have to sneak off?" I asked. Serafina had been annoying enough when she was present, now more of a nuisance when absent.

We went back to the dining room, and I made a general announcement.

"We can't find Serafina anywhere. We'll have to organise a search party of the castle and grounds. But first, it might be useful to find out who saw her last?"

I couldn't help but look at Austin at this juncture. He appeared unconcerned.

"Austin and I went to bed together around two in the morning," piped up Rosemary. I looked at her in surprise. She obviously understood my suspicions and felt no compunction in admitting that she had slept with Austin. There was more to Rosemary than I had thought. Perhaps, she had Austin's measure and still cared for him.

"I danced the jitterbug with her," volunteered Theo.

"Did anyone see her afterwards?" I asked. There was silence in the room.

"Let's organise a search," said Richard, standing up, prepared to take charge as the master of the household. He sent off pairs to each part of the castle and also the grounds.

Cecilia was looking upset. She hadn't been keen on Serafina in the first place, and now her engagement celebration was to be marred by this drama.

Forty minutes later, everyone assembled in the dining room. No one had found her.

"Do you think she went out early for a walk on the moors and has got lost?" asked Gertrude.

"Or perhaps a midnight swim in the loch?" suggested Theo.

"I suppose we could organise a search party of the moor on horseback," I said hesitantly. It seemed unlikely that Serafina would go out walking. She was not the type to engage in outdoor activities.

"We couldn't get into that room at the end of the corridor where the guest bedrooms are," said Ernest. "It was locked, and there was no key."

"That is strange," said Mummy. "There's no reason for it to be locked. It's a box room, storing nothing of value. It's never been locked, as far as I know."

She hurried out of the room to check, returning with a frown creasing her forehead.

"Richard, that room is locked, and there is no key. Did you lock it by any chance?"

"No, of course not," said Richard. "I do remember there being a key in the lock, but I've never turned it. I'll go and see if Cook has a spare. Otherwise, we'll break in."

Ann and I exchanged glances. This situation was getting spooky. For the first time, it occurred to me, that there might have been foul play. I hoped that Serafina's dead and battered body wasn't going to be found inside that small room. It would do our reputation no good at all.

Cook produced a bunch of miscellaneous keys that had accumulated over the years. Richard went upstairs to try them. Mummy, Ann, Henry and I hurried in his wake.

The tenth key that Richard tried turned the lock. The door opened inwards. Ann and I hung back. I was afraid of what we might find. Richard went in first, with Mummy behind him. The electric light wouldn't turn on. There was no bulb in the socket.

"That is very odd. I was in here yesterday. I remember turning the light on," said Mummy. She went over to the small window and drew back the thick curtains that probably hadn't been opened in years. The room was dusty. The big trunk with the dressing-up clothes was in the corner, but it was covered in blankets.

"I think someone has put her body in the trunk," I said in hushed tones.

Richard didn't hang back in horror. He pulled off the blankets and undid the clasp. Ann and I were peeping over his shoulder.

"She's there," said Ann in hushed and horrified tones.

Richard pulled her out. Her body was limp. Mummy felt for her pulse in her neck.

"She's alive, thank you, God," she cried.

Richard carried her out to the corridor. Mummy rushed ahead and opened the door to the blue room.

"Lay her on the bed," she said.

We crowded around. Mummy pulled the flimsy green skirt down and put a coverlet over her.

"Is there any sign of injury?" asked Ann anxiously. "Henry, you should examine her. I think a vet is the next best thing to a doctor."

"I'll call the real doctor," said Mummy and hurried out.

"She's got a lump on the back of her head," said Richard, "no blood, just a lump."

"Someone hit her over the head and threw her in the trunk," I said disbelievingly.

"Who would have done that?" asked Henry as he came in.

"Perhaps it would be easier to write down a list of people who had no reason to want to kill her," I replied. "I know that I wouldn't make it on that list. But it wasn't me," I added hastily.

"We don't know that someone actually wanted to kill her," said Mummy. "It may just have been a practical joke that went wrong."

"Pretty drastically wrong!" I exclaimed, thinking of the blankets piled on top of the trunk.

At this point Ernest burst into the room.

"Serafina! Serafina!" he cried. She fluttered her eyelids.

"Look, she's coming around!" I said. "She can tell us what happened."

Serafina blinked. Her round blue orbs looked at us with an uncomprehending unfocused gaze.

"If she has a concussion, then she needs quiet," said Mummy. "Don't badger her with questions. Richard, draw the curtains, and I think Ernest and I should stay here with her and the rest of you skedaddle. Jill, go downstairs and wait for the doctor and bring him up as soon as he arrives."

"Perhaps we should lock the box room," I suggested, trying to think like a detective. "There may be important clues in there. The scene needs to be preserved."

Mummy and Richard looked at each other helplessly.

"I'll lock the door," agreed Richard.

We left and went back to the library.

"I'll get Cook to bring up some tea and biscuits," said Ann.

"We need sustenance. I'll come with you," I said.

We hurried down to the kitchen. Cook wasn't around, so we set to making an enormous pot of tea. I raided the pantry and found rock buns, a gingerbread cake, shortbread and a batch of pumpkin scones wrapped in a tea towel.

"Milk, sugar, butter, jam and cream," said Ann. We piled up four trays.

Henry came in to offer to help.

"What do you think happened?" Ann asked.

"She upset someone to the point that they biffed her on the head and threw her in the trunk," I suggested.

"Do you think they would have got her out, or they intended to leave her there, hoping that we wouldn't find her. She would wither away and be a dried skeleton?" said Ann hesitantly.

"It doesn't bear thinking about," said Henry.

"But we have to think about it," I insisted. "Should we call the police?"

"Oh, dear. That would put the dampeners on poor Cecilia's party," said Ann.

"Not to mention the reputation of Blainstock Castle," I added. "Although perhaps we could do murder mystery weekends."

"Yes, but they're meant to be pretend, not real," said Ann.

"There's no way you're going to be able to hush this up," said Henry. "We'll just have to hope that there's an innocuous explanation and Serafina can tell us what happened when she can talk."

"In the meantime, can we keep the drama at bay. We'll tell everyone she's been found, that she had fallen and was unconscious," I suggested.

"I'm not sure that people will be satisfied with that. You know how everyone wants every gory detail," said Ann.

"Let's at least try," I cried, now desperate to keep it under wraps.

We carried the trays upstairs. We had forgotten cups and saucers and plates and had to go back to the kitchen.

"I think we need to make a list of all the people who might have reason to want to hurt Serafina," said Ann in hushed tones.

"Alright, but first, I need some food. I'm famished, and I can't think properly when I'm hungry. As soon as everything is set out in the library, let's go up with cups of tea for Mummy, Ernest and hopefully Serafina. See if we can find out what she is saying."

At that moment, Dr Micklejohn arrived. He was tall and gaunt.

I took him upstairs. He went into the bedroom and firmly shut the door in my face. A few moments later, Ernest came out.

"What is she saying?" I hissed at him.

"She can't remember anything," he replied.

This was the worst-case scenario. There was no way she had fallen over, hit her head and then locked herself in the trunk. There had definitely been foul play.

"We think it best not to tell everyone. Just to say she was unconscious, and now we've found her," I said.

"Alright," agreed Ernest. "But who could have done this to her?"

I thought that would be a long list, but I didn't say it out loud.

"Come down to the library and have some tea," I suggested. "But remember, mum's the word."

Ann came up the stairs at that moment with some tea.

"I don't think it's the right time," I said. "Just put the tray down outside the door. Let's go back and attend to the guests."

"She can't remember anything," I muttered to Ann as we followed the dejected and worried Ernest to the library.

The room was full of guests who were bubbling over with excitement and relief and demanding details.

"She's been found. She was unconscious but come round now. The doctor is with her, and until she remembers, we don't know exactly what happened," I announced to the room at large. Cecilia bustled up to me.

"But Jill, *where* was she found?" she demanded.

"In the box room at the end of the corridor of guest rooms," I said, missing out the significant details that the room had been locked, the key missing, and the latches on the trunk closed. I looked around. It would be very unlikely that a stranger had done this. One of the people in this room was the attacker. Perhaps they were going to strike again? I looked at Ann and it seemed to me that she was thinking the same thing.

"Jill, let's go down to the kitchen and make another pot of tea," she said, shooting me a meaningful look.

"I'll come with you," said Henry. I suddenly wished that Frank was here. I was sure that with his sharp brain we could come up with an answer to this mystery. I felt a huge desire to run over to the Dower House to confide in him.

*****

The atmosphere on Sunday night was subdued. The gaiety of the previous evening had dissolved like dirty bathwater down the plug hole. Everyone would be leaving on the following day, and presumably, our attacker amongst them would get clean away. Although, we did know who everyone was and where they lived.

Ann and I sat up in our beds compiling lists of suspects."

"I think that Susan Pyke, well, King now, has got to be the prime suspect," said Ann. "We know that she and Austin had been a thing. She was totally mad about him and it was no secret that she was hoping he would suggest she leave her husband and they marry. Poor thing. I think she totally miscalculated the motives of Austin. I don't think he is the marrying kind."

"But what about him and the Hon Rosemary? She seems a decent and sensible young woman. She is hooked up with Austin. She even admitted that they were sleeping together on the night. Not that that is total evidence he didn't stuff Serafina in the trunk. He could have met up with her in the corridor, lured her into the box room and done the deed, then back to bed with Rosemary."

"Yes, that's true," I said slowly. "But I don't see what Austin would have to gain from such a deed?"

"The other major question is, were they attempting to murder Serafina or just give her a big fright? Do you think she knows who it was and won't say, through fear, or perhaps covering up some nefarious deeds?"

"Let's write that down. Was it just assault, or was it attempted murder?" I asked.

"If they wanted to murder her, then, surely, they would have done the job properly before putting her in the trunk. Perhaps we can assume it was just an attack," said Ann.

"If we hadn't found her, they would have given us an anonymous tip," I said thoughtfully. "You know, I think we've got to get in and talk to Serafina. Mummy has been firm that she shouldn't be bothered, but I suspect she knows more than what she says. Why else would she not want the police to investigate?"

"Do you think Rosemary wanted to give her a summary lesson not to flirt so outrageously with her boyfriend?" asked Ann. "That might be why she told us that she had slept with Austin. To give herself an alibi."

"Yes, but surely hitting her over the head and locking her in a trunk is more than paying her back for some tasteless flirtation."

"Well, that's Susan King at the top of the list, then perhaps Rosemary. I hate to cast aspersions, but she was pretty brutal with Dinah. She called her a 'jumped-up guttersnipe'. I'm not sure that something surreptitious is Dinah's style, but she's got to go on the list."

"So far, we've got females. What about men? Do you think Simon Caxton-Thorpe would have been defending Dinah's honour?" Ann suggested.

"We'll put him down as well then, but he seems like a bit of a wimp," I said.

"Do you know if she's upset Lavender and Morgan. A prank like this is a trifle childish and look what Ruby did when she dyed Porsche's horse green. Young girls are quite capable of being ruthless," said Ann.

"She could easily have made some insulting and waspish comment towards them," I agreed. "But can we put them on the list, without any evidence?" I asked.

"We've only got motive for anyone. No evidence. Put them down. We can easily cross them off," replied Ann.

"We have to include Cecilia. Do you remember that Royce was infatuated with Serafina in the first place? She rejected him for Ernest, but I did notice that Cecilia was keeping a keen eye on her," I said, adding her name to the list.

"What about Bunty? She's a strange woman, the total opposite of Serafina. She could certainly have been the butt of her malice," suggested Ann.

"We can certainly put her down. She's just the sort of outsider that Serafina would have taken a swipe at," I agreed. "You know there are so many people who would like to have seen Serafina get her comeuppance that we could be looking at a *Murder on the Orient Express* scenario. A whole group of people might have banded together to do the deed."

"Gosh!" said Ann. "That means it was happening right under our noses, and we were totally unaware."

"I was too upset about Cecilia's comment," I said dejectedly.

"What comment?" asked Ann.

For some reason, I did not want to confide in Ann. I think it was the first time in our relationship that I was holding back.

"Something and nothing. You know how annoying and tactless Cecilia can be," I said off-handedly.

"Why don't we go and visit Serafina now? Everyone else is in bed. We could say we thought we heard her cry out, and we were going to check on her," suggested Ann.

"Are you thinking we finish the job and smother her with a pillow," I said flippantly.

"Don't joke," said Ann. "We'll be each other's witness if we find her dead in bed."

"Oh no," I said, appalled. "The castle's reputation will be forever smirched if that is the case."

We pulled on our dressing gowns and taking the torch I always kept by my bedside, we crept through the corridors, starting at every tiny noise. It is pretty amazing just how many rustles and creaks there are in an old castle.

We tiptoed down the guest room corridor and came to the blue door. Cautiously we turned the handle and went in. A single beam of moonlight shone through a gap in the curtains revealing Serafina's pretty face. She was sound asleep.

"I don't think we should wake her up," whispered Ann. "She looks so peaceful. I imagine she needs her sleep."

At that moment, perhaps disturbed by our whispered conversation, she stirred.

"Serafina, are you alright?" I asked.

She made some indistinguishable murmuring noises. We stood looking at her. She opened her eyes and saw us and screeched a little. I feared she was going to wake everyone in the surrounding rooms.

"Serafina, it's me and Ann," I said soothingly. She struggled up, sitting in bed looking around wildly. "We thought we heard you call out," I lied through my teeth, feeling an utter fraud.

"I don't know. Perhaps it was a bad dream," said Serafina, looking confused.

"Can you remember what happened to you?" I asked.

"No, no!" she cried. "It's all a fug."

"What can you remember? What's the last thing you remembered from that night?"

"I was dancing with Ernest and then with that rustic man dressed up as a witch. He was a terrible dancer. I went upstairs to the bathroom. I fixed my makeup, and then everything went blank. Perhaps someone hit me over the head as I came out, dragged me to the end of the corridor and put me in the trunk."

She was weeping now, pathetic little sobs of despair. I felt ashamed, putting her through this.

"You have no sense of whether it was a man or a woman, one or perhaps two people?" asked Ann persistently.

"No, nothing. It's just a blank. They must have hit me on the head, and then it is nothing," she replied.

"Go back to sleep. I hope we haven't disturbed you," I said.

We crept back to my bedroom.

"Do you think she is hiding something?" I asked.

"I don't know. Perhaps she is just genuinely suffering amnesia due to the hit on the back of the head," Ann replied.

"I hope we haven't further harmed her," I said.

*****

On Monday morning, guests came downstairs with their bags packed. Everyone was talking in hushed tones. There was no sign of Serafina.

"I wonder whether we shouldn't have called the police," said Mummy to me as we helped Cook in the kitchen with the breakfast platters.

"What exactly did Serafina say?" I asked.

"She said she didn't want a fuss. She just wanted to forget it had ever happened. I don't think she is telling us everything. But, there is something Jill. I showed it to Richard and we didn't know what to do. It was a note in Serafina's pocket. Here look." She showed me a scrap of paper. On it was written in block capitals. "MEET ME IN THE BOX ROOM AT THE END OF THE BEDROOM CORRIDOR, LOVE A."

"That means it was an assignation," I exclaimed. "A. that is probably Austin. A. Surely not Aggie!"

"It doesn't mean it was Austin who gave her the note. Obviously, it was a lure. Perhaps that is why she doesn't want to talk to the police about it.

Her carrying on with Austin does not put her in a good light," reasoned Mummy.

"So, she wasn't hit on the head as she came out of the bathroom. She walked down the corridor to the box room. That would explain the fact that the light bulb was unscrewed. She went in. It was dark, and they biffed her over the head, then stuffed her into the trunk."

*****

The guests left. The large Talbot and Pevensy contingent who were travelling by rail was taken to the station to catch the ten o'clock train. Richard and Hugh drove them to the station and then returned for the mountains of luggage. It had been agreed that Serafina would stay a few days to make sure she had recovered from her concussion.

The black Bentley had only four people leaving: Ernest, Simon Caxton-Thorpe, Dinah Dean and Rosemary Dill. While Ernest and Simon were packing the suitcases in the trunk, I drew Dinah aside.

"Dinah, you're the brains of the bunch in this group. Who do you think it was that shoved Serafina in the trunk?"

She looked at me, not bothering to dispute the statement that she might be the most intelligent.

"I'll ask you a question," she replied enigmatically. "Did you know that Serafina and Rosemary were acquainted with one another before they came to this party? They are not on good terms. There were several waspish exchanges when we travelled up here."

"So, you are saying that it might have been Rosemary?" I asked.

"Not exactly. I think that the puzzle is more complicated. Rosemary and Hetty Silverthorne were good friends. They go way back. So, the other question is how did it come about that Hetty came up to photograph the guests. That should give you something to work on," she said, smiling a Madonna smile. "Jill the Journalist, turns into Jill the Detective."

"Sometimes I think you don't take me seriously," I quipped.

She grinned at me.

We waved them off. This was a new thought. The relationship between Rosemary and Serafina and the possible alliance between Rosemary and Hetty. Ann and I hadn't even considered Hetty. She'd left to go back to London, and we hadn't thought of putting her on the list of suspects. She was far too hard-bitten to be offended by any spiteful little comments that might have been directed at her.

I hurried off to find Ann. She had asked Henry if they could stay another day, but he had said he absolutely had to get back to Oxfordshire. She was stuffing her clothes into a bag in my bedroom.

"Ann, I've just talked to Dinah. She says that Rosemary and Serafina knew each other and didn't get on, and that Rosemary and Hetty might have been in cahoots together. It's up to you to continue to investigate when you get back to Oxfordshire and see what you can discover. I can keep an eye on Serafina and hope that she says something else. I can show her the note and see if that brings on some more recall."

"That sounds interesting," said Ann. "I liked Rosemary. Of course, she had the motive of Serafina going after her boyfriend, but perhaps there is history there. Hetty! Now she's a very bold, ruthless person and I imagine she would be a loyal friend. I'm not sure how to tackle her. I would have to think up a ruse to seek her out. She's not likely to let anything slip."

I waved goodbye to Henry and Ann and thought I needed to go to the stables to do some work. Frank would probably be there. He had said we needed to talk but to avoid that conversation, I would tell him all about the Serafina in the Trunk affair.

Linda, Hugh and John had finished the mucking out and had put some of the horses out in the small fields.

"Are you riding Balius or Shadow this morning?" asked John. "If not, we can put them out in the field."

"I think I'll take Balius for a hack," I said. "I'll put Shadow out."

I needed to get out in the open air and let the dark shadows and suspicions clouding my brain clear. I needed to think. I have always found that thinking is much easier on horseback.

There was no sign of Frank, but Yola was bumping around the outside arena on Skydiver. I averted my eyes. The morning was clear, the air fresh, and the sky arched above me. I tried to clear my mind and focus on Balius. He was going so well these days. He had come on wonderfully. He stepped out briskly with a long, low stride. I began to ponder my past idea before the Serafina event occurred. I wanted Balius to show the world his talents this summer. If I did have to stay up in Scotland, then I would have to find out about the big shows up here. If we had two working pupils this summer, they could do a lot of the riding schoolwork, especially if Linda was tripping off to Europe with the Laskeys. I would get my BSJA membership and try some Foxhunter competitions. I was inspired by Charles Ravenscroft when he came up as a prize winner.

I trotted around the loch and set off up the hill towards the moorland. Balius was restive, flicking his ears and looking backwards. It was Frank and Firestorm trotting up behind us.

"Hi, Jill!" called Frank, "they told me that you had set off ten minutes before me."

"Riding the red monster again," I said.

"Yes, Jack declared he had paperwork to do this morning."

"Reading the newspaper," I suggested. We laughed together.

"Did you hear about what happened to Serafina Collins?" I asked.

"There were whispers. I understand that she got herself knocked out."

"Well, it was a bit more than that. She was biffed over the head and stuffed into a trunk and locked in there. The door of the box room was locked as well. The key missing."

"Gosh! That's a bit dramatic. Do you know who did it?"

"Not really. There are suspects. Quite a lot of them. Ann and I have tried our hand at detecting. We didn't call the police. It seems she was lured into the box room with a note that was supposedly from Austin Pevensy."

"I thought Austin's girlfriend was Rosemary. She seemed like a decent sort," said Frank.

"Austin is a playboy. He plays fast and loose with any woman's affections if she's stupid enough to fall for him. We wondered if it might have been Susan King who got upset with Serafina. She was hot on Austin, and it seems he's thrown her over."

"What a complicated life some people lead," said Frank disapprovingly. I was pleased with his strait-laced attitude.

We rode on in silence. I thought of telling him about the lead with Rosemary and Hetty, but I sensed that he was not interested. It occurred to me then that we might never know who had done this to Serafina. Perhaps it wasn't important. Not compared with the fact that Frank and I needed to talk about our relationship. He didn't bring up the subject. Presumably, it was a conversation that wouldn't take place on horseback.

*****

A week later, two packets arrived by post. One was from London, with no sender's name or address. It was a key. There was no need to rush upstairs to try it in the lock. Undoubtedly it was the key to the box room. I held it up for Mummy and Richard to see. The silence crackled as if it were electric.

The second packet was several pages of writing from Ann. I took it into the library to read in privacy.

31ˢᵗ May 1962

Pool Cottage

Chatton

Dear Jill,

What a tale I have to tell and from what I shall write we can draw some conclusions, but there is no proof, or evidence that could be used to convict anyone.

I have asked around and finally came upon an acquaintance who knows the Hon Rosemary Dill and her family. They have suffered some catastrophic blows in the last few years. Rosemary's younger sister, Flora, was eighteen years old when she married an older man, Captain La Fontaine. She was besotted with this dashing and handsome officer and although her family thought her too young to wed, they could not withstand her pleading and there was a grand wedding with all the county invited.

Flora was a delicate young beauty, too romantic for her own good and innocent of the wiles of an unscrupulous older man. She became pregnant within two months of the marriage. They lived in a small house in a remote village in Devonshire. Her family did not have much contact with her. Then, the news came to them that she had died by her own hand, pregnant, alone in the cottage. Apparently, she had drunk cleaning fluid. Rosemary and her mother dashed to the village and arranged for the body to be returned to Oxfordshire for the burial.

The affair was reported in the local newspaper and also was mentioned in the London papers due to the shocking nature of the matter and the aristocratic connections of the Dill family. Apparently, it was Hetty Silverthorne who investigated and wrote the story. Captain La Fontaine had been in London at the time of his wife's death. He attended the funeral and then inherited Flora's wealth, which was a considerable sum settled on her at the time of her marriage. It had been left to her by her maternal grandmother who wished her grand-daughters to have some financial independence when they became married women.

What was not written about in the official accounts was that Captain La Fontaine had been cavorting around town with another young woman who was – you guessed it – Serafina Collins. News of the affair had reached Flora who was alone in Devonshire, without the support of her family, and could not bear the shame and distress, and took her own life.

Dinah was correct when she pointed you in the direction of Rosemary and Hetty. I think that brings this matter to a close. We can, perhaps, look forward to some disaster falling upon Captain La Fontaine but I think it is best that a line be drawn under the matter.

I hope that all of you at the castle are recovering from the dramatic events of the house party. I saw Cecilia the other day in Oxford and she is going from strength to strength, taking to her role as Duchess-in-waiting like a duck to water. She told me that Austin and Rosemary, perhaps surprisingly, continue to be a young couple out and about on the Oxfordshire social circuit (?!).

Henry and I have decided that I won't go to Bristol to study veterinary science. We are secretly planning to wed at the end of summer, but it has not yet been announced, so please don't tell anyone, except Frank, your mother and Richard, all who can be trusted. We thought we might stay on at Pool Cottage if that is agreeable to you. Of course, if you were to return to live in Oxfordshire and want the cottage back, we shall make other arrangements. Eventually we will buy our own place and construct, or convert, a building to be an animal surgery.

So much is happening, talk soon.

Your loving friend, Ann.

THE END

True Love in Oxfordshire

Narrated by Susan Barington-Brown

What I love most about my darling Charles is that he is always coming up with the most original and interesting ideas. Finally, finally, he had finished his exams. His schooling had been delayed when he was sick with poliomyelitis, so he was a year behind. We were the same age, but I had finished school the year before.

Now, we had a long leisurely summer ahead of us. Charles was waiting for his results before he went up to Oxford to study to become a solicitor. I had invited him to come and stay at Basset Towers for a few days. On the first afternoon of his arrival, we escaped from my mother and elder sister, Valerie. We sat under the oak tree in the garden, having tea.

"I was thinking of writing detective stories," he told me. "It's something I might have a go at this summer, now my schooldays are behind me, and I'm waiting to go up. I love the way you have to plot them out, know the answer from the beginning and work backwards. I've just been reading this wizard story with Sherlock Holmes where he is investigating the murder of a trainer and the disappearance of a top racehorse."

"I'm sure you'll make a huge success of it. You get such good ideas. I think having horses in a detective story would make it extremely interesting. I wish I could do something like that. I'm such a flibberty-gibbert," I said admiringly.

It had been Charles who had come up with an idea for my own future career, and it had been brilliant. We had been up at Blainstock Castle for a fortnight with four other prize winners competing for the grand prize of a weekend trip to the Spanish Riding School in Vienna, which neither of us had won.

One of the competitions had been to design a showjump. I've always loved making jumps, so this was right up my street. Then Charles put two things together, my father has a shoe manufacturing business, and I have a flair for designing, so why didn't I work in the factory designing shoes? Not just ordinary brown or black lace-ups, but fantabulous, splangly and gorgeous shoes, and even better, boots.

"You know that we've been invited to go out with Henry and Noel to celebrate next Saturday night," I told him. "We're to go to the Blue Jackdaw! We'll be like proper grown-ups!"

"That sounds very sophisticated," said Charles. "I mean they're very horsey-type people. I didn't think they would go to a jazz club like that."

"I thought it would be fun. I've never been to a jazz club. Have you?" I asked.

"No," admitted Charles.

"Well, I'm not sure that they have either, but Noel was talking to me the other day, saying that she was determined to widen her horizons, step out of the narrow boundaries of her life, experience new things. She says it will be good for Henry as the army is making him like an automaton. So, I guess a jazz club is a good beginning. I mean, it's not like going to live in Istanbul for a year or anything like that, is it?"

I dressed carefully on the night of our Blue Jackdaw outing. I was a little anxious about Charles and this first meeting with Noel and Henry. I utterly adored him, and I was sure that Noel would like him, but Henry was a different kettle of fish. He was an odd mixture of an upright British public schoolboy, an aspiring officer in the army but still a horse-crazy boy who could easily descend into the depths of depression when his horse wasn't going well.

When it came to deciding what to wear, I had firmly ignored any suggestions from Mummy and Valerie, who had the most execrable dress sense. I went for something plain, simple and hopefully elegant - the ubiquitous little black dress. I embellished the outfit with a bright jade-green necklace that Daddy had brought back from Asia on one of his business trips.

Charles arrived to pick me up. He wore a pair of smart trousers and a jacket that wasn't the routine tweed but a snazzy blue and silver-grey chequered pattern. I invited him in, and we sat alone in the dining room to partake of a light supper. Then, we set out in Charles' flashy little sports car, which his parents had given him to celebrate his finishing school. Charles opened the door for me with an impressive flourishing gesture. I giggled and remembered to do the debutante legs together move to get into my seat.

We drove off in high spirits. I felt like we were the most glamorous couple in the world. The first beings to ever discover the effervescent fizz of being in love.

The Blue Jackdaw was a notorious jazz club in Oxford, rumoured to be the hangout of London underworld characters who needed to get out of the city because the heat was on. I had been told that they wore lots of heavy gold rings to denote the number of hits they had made.

We met Henry and Noel in the car park and trooped in together. We were instantly enveloped in a smoky fug. It was like London must have been in the days of the Great Smog. The smell of mingled stale and fresh cigarette smoke, with a mixture of heady perfumes, was overwhelming. I tottered cautiously, teetering on my high heels that made me nearly as tall as Charles. I could make out a number of small round tables and chairs in the centre in front of the stage. Around the room's perimeter were alcoves scooped out of the walls ringed by upholstered red velvet banquettes and small circular tables for drinks, ashtrays and candles. It was deliciously raffish, and I shivered in delight. Plans for skulduggery hung like miasmas in the air around us.

"I think we should sit right in the middle. We don't want to miss anything," said Henry in a bossy voice. Obviously, the army was having an effect. He was practising his leading and marshalling skills.

Obediently, the rest of us followed him and pulled up chairs around the little table. Three candles were flickering in the centre. A girl dressed in the French burlesque style slid over to us, offering packets of cigarettes that were set out on her tray. Then, a waitress approached and took our orders. Charles and I asked for lemonade, and Henry and Noel had gin and tonics.

"I've been so looking forward to meeting you, Charles," said Noel.

"And I you, both of you," replied Charles.

"That two weeks at Blainstock sounded interesting," said Henry. "Mark Lansdowne was telling me about it."

"It was fab," I said. "Such lovely people up there. And to meet the famous Jill Crewe was so interesting. Next time she's in Oxfordshire, I want to invite her to a house party for the weekend." I had been reading some books set in the 1920s when people went off to house parties and balls all the time.

"There's Ann Derry over there with Henry Thurston if you're interested," said Henry, nodding in the direction of a table at the edge of the cluster, in a voice that suggested that the Chattonites were no better than those from West Barsetshire.

"Oh, how fantastic. You know them!" I exclaimed, "Please do introduce us. I've been dying to meet them since I read Jill's books." I wasn't going to pander to Henry's superior tone and continued to show an enthusiasm approaching hero-worship for all the Chattonite horsey people.

Obviously, I'm not the most tactful of people, but I dislike Henry when he gets that superior twist on his face. According to Jill's books, Ann was a merry soul, and she looked just as she was described, with a smiling, jolly round face and a cap of shiny curly red hair.

"Let's get our drinks first," said Noel. "We don't want to look like autograph hunters."

"Quite right," said Henry. "A measure of social reserve is called for."

Charles nodded in agreement.

A singer came onto the stage, which was a raised dais at the end of the room. She began to sing in a husky voice. She was rather plump, with short dark hair cut in a shiny bob, which gave her the look of a Dutch doll. Her dress was a deep claret colour, shimmery, with a low neckline. Her eyebrows were shaped like half-moons, thick and arched over eyes made up with dark purple smudged eyelids and thick black lashes that must be false. Her luscious lips were painted in the exact shade of the dress. She was strumming a ukulele.

Behind her was a theatrical backdrop: a crescent moon filled with red silk flowers and striped dark purple and dull gold curtains. A suited man was playing the saxophone and another man was seated behind with an acoustic guitar.

"Noel, would you like to dance?" asked Henry.

"Certainly," said Noel.

"We'll sit it out, I think," I said, not wanting Charles to have to explain that he couldn't dance. After his poliomyelitis, he had been left with a limpy leg.

Noel and Henry were the only couple on the floor, and they fitted together like pieces in a jigsaw puzzle. Then Ann and the other Henry sashayed onto the floor. I was able to stare and stare to my heart's content. Once the set was over, Noel and Charles asked them to join us at the table, and I felt my happiness was complete.

Introductions were made, and the waitress brought over Ann and Henry's drinks. It was crowded around our little table.

"We're celebrating me *finally* finishing my exams," said Ann. "You know I went back to school to qualify for university entrance."

"It's the same with Charles. He just finished," I chipped in.

"Are any of you going to the horse show being held in Birtle in a couple of weeks?" asked Ann, blithely flipping from one topic to another.

"I hadn't thought," I exclaimed. "What type of events?"

Ann opened her clutch purse and produced a schedule, like a magician pulling a bunny out of a hat.

"Isn't she marvellous," commented Henry, watching his beloved with unalloyed approval.

Noel and I pored over the paper. It was hard to read in the dim candlelight.

"There are the usual riding, pony and hack classes, including pairs," I said. "Noel, you and I could ride Tranquil and Truant in the Pair of Lady Hacks."

"Yes, that would work," said Noel. "Truant is going rather well at the moment. So, I thought I might also enter him in a jumping class."

"Yes, Tranquil jumped very well at Blainstock," I said. "Henry, are you riding Echo?"

"Yes. Finch has been lunging him regularly, and Christo comes up and rides him at least twice a week while I've been away," replied Henry.

"Chisto!" gasped Noel.

"Yes, she's come on marvellously, you know," said Henry heedlessly. "She and Dragonfly have had private lessons from some dressage coach, and she's easily as good as you now, Noel."

"Charles, you must jump Secret," I interjected hastily.

"My Henry is more an aficionado of cross-country, hunter trials, but you could have a bash at showjumping," said Ann.

"Bash would probably be the word for it, but I'll have a go," said Henry equitably.

"What horse are you riding at the moment, Ann?" I asked curiously. In the last book I'd read, she'd been hacking around the lanes on Black Comedy, a battle-scarred old steeplechaser.

"I'll come along and be the groom and run around and get numbers for you all," said Ann cheerfully. "I've gone off competing these days."

"You can ride Dauntless in something if you want," suggested Henry.

"No, darling. That's frightfully kind, but my competitive spirit has evaporated into the atmosphere."

We all sipped our drinks for a moment.

"Gosh! Look at that woman who has just walked in. She's standing over there by that table with London gangsters," said Ann, whose merry eyes were constantly darting here and there.

The woman had long hair all the way to her hips, perfectly straight and shining like the moon, as colourless as flax. Her eyes were the colour of cold Scandinavian sky, her skin as pale as pearl, and she glowed like an undersea creature, edged with phosphorescence swirling around her.

"She would make a wonderful character in my detective novel," said Charles. "She must be involved in the underworld, the perfect foil to those colourful rough-edged criminals."

"Why don't you go over and interview them? I understand that it is considered chic to have a tame gangster invited to one's parties," Henry said with a disdainful note.

"Henry!" exclaimed Noel. "Don't be like that. She *is* an intriguing creature."

"Shall I ask her to dance?" suggested Henry truculently.

Noel looked mulish. I feared that they weren't getting on very well. They seemed to be growing away from each other. It was strange. In West Barsetshire Pony Club, everyone had thought that they were made for each other.

"As far as Birtle Show goes, I think there'll be a good attendance from the Chatton contingent," said Ann tactfully changing the subject. "I know that Wendy Mead is going to be jumping Bright Eyes in the novice class. Lavender Ellison-Heath has this gorgeous new show pony called Summer Fancy, and there's a rising star, young Lettie Tregarth on Cornish Boy."

The singer returned to the stage and began crooning a slow, sad song.

"I think I might be able to manage this one," Charles said. "Susan, would you like to dance?"

"Oh, yes, please." I was relieved to be able to leave the table where Henry's bad temper had spoiled the convivial atmosphere. Instead, we propped each other up on the dance floor and swayed romantically to the sad, haunting music.

We left soon after that.

"I'm not sure that Henry Thornton is going to be my best friend," said Charles in the car.

"I think the issue is more with Henry and the world at large," I replied. "Perhaps the army isn't all that he thought it might be. Did you see Noel's face when he said that Christo was as good as rider as her?"

"What was that about?" asked Charles.

"Christo is a very old friend of Henry's, growing up as kids. She's nice, very jolly hockey sticks, no-nonsense, athletic, rides, swims, plays tennis."

"Then what is the problem?" asked Charles, genuinely puzzled. I smiled at him. He was so wonderfully straightforward. It was one of the things that I loved about him.

"What did you think of Ann and Henry-the-vet?" I asked, changing the subject.

"I liked them," said Charles. "She is such a merry soul, and he seems like a good egg. If Secret develops a strange disease, I might get him to look at her."

"Birtle Show should be fun, the first in the season," I said. "You'll have to sharpen up Secret."

"She's been staying at Claire's at Eastbridge during my last term, and she will have been keeping her up to the mark," he replied.

"It's going to be such fun going around the shows this summer," I chirped. "I'll be able to pick you up in the horse box, and we can set up camp, like playing house."

*****

Charles went home after a couple of wonderful days together. Then, I resolved to begin my preparations for Birtle Show. I had been rather lacksadaisical in my training recently. Working most days in the shoe factory, I had spent the late afternoons hacking through the lanes, dreaming about shoe design. So, I decided to do some flat work. I was hoping that the instruction I had received at Blainstock Riding Stables would stand me in good stead. Tranquil was his usual good-natured self, and we trotted and cantered some circles. I wished that Noel was there with suggestions, schooling on my own was boring, and I was uninspired.

I let Tranquil stay out in the field that evening. The weather was warm, and I felt that it would be a nice treat for him. I leaned on the gate, watching him walk slowly away, picking at a tuft of grass here or there. He raised his head and searched the horizon. Then he neighed at the horses that were grazing two fields away. I knew that it wasn't right for him to always be alone. Horses were gregarious animals and needed company. I didn't think that I would have enough time to ride a second horse. Bob was a very efficient groom, but I didn't like him riding Tranquil as he was a very rough rider. A retired horse that needed a good home would be perfect. I would contact Noel to see if she knew of any.

Noel sounded very gloomy when I rang.

"What's the matter?" I asked.

Henry has invited me over to Radney Manor for several days. I'm to take Truant and he wants us to school together.

"But I thought that you would be thrilled to spend some time with him, and Radney Manor is a very pleasant house to stay in," I reasoned. The house was grand, part ancient monastery and part Tudor manor, sheltering in the lee of a hill. It was filled with interesting objects and had wonderful views over the village of Radney. There was even a suit of armour in the hall and an antique model cannon displayed in the drawing room.

"It's Henry. He's changed, and I'm not sure I like his new personality. He seems very bossy and critical, and it's awkward," replied Noel.

Privately, I thought Henry had always been like that, but tactfully I changed the subject.

"I had wanted to ask you to come over and school with me," I said. "I made a desultory effort at circle work on Tranquil this afternoon, but I can never really tell whether he is going well or not. I need your keen eye upon me."

"I've got an idea!" exclaimed Noel. "I'll suggest to Henry that you come as well. Then, perhaps Bob can take both our horses over in the horse box."

"Do you think Henry will mind me coming as well?" I asked.

"I don't see that he'll object," said Noel.

"But I rather wanted to spend some time with Charles," I said hesitantly.

"I know. I'll ask Henry if you can both come. We can all school the horses together. I will feel much better with other people around, especially another chap for Henry. He might be craving masculine company as he's got used to being in the army."

I was a little doubtful and reluctantly agreed that Noel should broach the subject with Henry. If he said no, I would be happy to forget the idea.

Noel rang the next day to give me the bad news that Henry had agreed that we should all come. His mother was pleased that he had friends to stay as his sister, Elisabeth was going abroad with friends, and his father was away on a business trip. She liked the house to be filled with lively people.

"Well, that's settled. I shall ring Charles. When shall we go?" I asked.

"The plan is to get there tomorrow afternoon and stay for only two nights. If it all gets too much, then we won't be stuck there forever."

"I'm sure everything between you and Henry will get back to the way it was," I said soothingly. "Charles and I will model the behaviour of a happy couple, and he can take his cue from that."

"You're the eternal optimist, Susan," replied Noel.

*****

Charles wasn't filled with enthusiasm at the idea of staying at Radney Manor, but he said his parents were thrilled that he was being invited. They had been worried that he was growing solitary and peculiar. Now, he had friends of his own age who shared his interests and wasn't it just working out splendidly?

Bob loaded Tranquil and we progressed to Noel's house, where we loaded Truant, and then twenty miles further away, we picked up Secret and Charles on the way to Henry's house. We were a merry band, the three of us sitting on the back seat of the horse truck, laughing and joking. I wished that it was just the three of us and the convivial atmosphere would not be spoiled by the disgruntled Henry. Then, I decided to believe that Henry would have got over his ill temper and would be an amusing and hospitable host.

Noel and I were sharing a room, and I saw that she was reading a book by Kipling.

"Remember that Henry was always quoting from something that Kipling wrote when we were young," I said.

"Yes. Other people thought he was a bit of a windbag, but there is one story that I absolutely adore. *The Maltese Cat* is told from the point of view of a polo pony. It is so interesting," said Noel. "You really should read it, Susan. I think you would enjoy it. Actually one of the ponies is called Gray Dawn, which was the name that June gave to her New Forest pony which she trained. Do you remember it was in a double bridle and miles behind the bit and doing flying changes in the front but not back. But they spelt it with the English version of Grey, 'ey' not 'ay'."

"Your eye for detail, even with spelling is amazing," I said admiringly.

The meals served at Radney Manor were reputed to be uninspiring at best. Tonight was no exception. There was very chewy cold mutton, a potato salad with no herbs or flavourings and not enough mayonnaise, hard-boiled eggs that had been overcooked to the point of being vulcanised, and a very pallid salad of wilted lettuce leaves. Most of the conversation was catching up on the news of the West Barsetshire Pony Club members.

"You know I was thinking this afternoon, about the olden days," began Henry.

"Reminiscing and nostalgia in our advanced old age," quipped Noel.

"Whatever happened to June Creswell? She just disappeared?" continued Henry, giving Noel a squashing look.

"I know! I know!" I tooted. "Mummy told me. She's gone to London to live with some cousins, and she's works in real estate. Apparently, she's an absolute shark and closes deals all day long."

"Who is June Creswell?" asked Charles, looking bewildered.

"She was the most awful girl. It was our first bonding experience. Do you remember Noel? We both hated her. She was so arrogant and put the rest of us down as if we were bugs to be squashed," I replied.

"Every pony club has to have at least one. I blame her mother more than anything. She did nothing but encourage her child to think she was better than everyone else," said Henry wisely.

"Did she really give up horses entirely?" asked Noel.

"Yes. She says she never wants anything to do with them again," I replied.

We all shook our heads in disbelief.

"I've just remembered," said Henry. "What happened in the inter-branch one-day event. Uncle George announced the long list at the end of last summer's camp. I know you competed, Noel, but I don't remember you writing with the results."

"Noel and I were on the team, and Gay Millwood and Christopher Minton," I replied. "Didn't Noel tell you? She won the individual, and we were third in the team event."

"You won! Noel! Well done! You're always hiding your light under a bushel," exclaimed Henry. "Uncle George must have been thrilled."

"He was rather pleased," admitted Noel, blushing red as a beetroot. "I think he felt that all his efforts to improve our dressage had paid off. A lot of the other teams were abysmal and just seemed to think that as long as they batted around the cross-country course, it would be fine."

"Dear Uncle George, he's very keen on dressage," said Henry.

"We had a chance to ride this amazing dressage horse at Blainstock," piped up Charles, probably thankful that he had something to contribute to the conversation. "You know that's where we met," he flashed a beaming smile at me. "This horse belonged to Jill Crewe, his name was Skydancer, and we each got the chance to do an advanced test on him. It was super. I had no idea that boring old flat work could be like that."

"Yes, I heard about that horse. Apparently, she did an exhibition on him at Chatton Show last summer. It's a shame that dressage hasn't been established in Britain. You know it's doubtful that we'll even be able to get a team together for the Olympics in the autumn," added Noel.

"Charles is planning on entering some more Foxhunter classes, this summer," I said proudly, wanting to skim over Charles' comment about 'boring old flat work'. He hadn't quite taken on board the concept of dressage being the basis of all good riding, which had been drummed into us at West Barsetshire for so many years.

"I must admit, I feel like an absolute beginner compared to you people," admitted my beloved. "You've all been riding for years, and I'm a raw beginner who just forged ahead to enter showjumping classes, not really understanding how much there was to learn."

"Yes, but you had the confidence and you qualified for the Foxhunter Championships," I went on.

"It really was beginner's luck," he said modestly.

"If you can do that well in your first season, then you're obviously extremely gifted," said Henry, looking impressed. "We've all been slogging around the pony club and gymkhana circuit for years and not got that far."

"Well, for me riding is always going to be a hobby. You know I'm off to London for a design course in the autumn, and I've been working in Daddy's factory, on the shop floor, getting some practical experience. Did I tell you, Henry, that I'm going to be a shoe fashion designer?"

"Fashion and frippery are merely a search for the next new absurdity," misquoted Henry in a superior way. "As far as my riding ambitions go, the army is pretty good. You know they give you time off if you want to compete at Badminton, Burghley, the European Championships or the Olympics," said Henry. "There is a strong tradition. You know Major General James Templer won Badminton this year, and he's off to Tokyo as a member of the British eventing team in the autumn."

"Hopefully, I'm going up to Oxford this autumn, and I can still live at home and ride and keep competing in the summer," said Charles.

"That leaves you, Noel," I said. "I know you hunt all through the winter, and you're still involved in West Barsetshire Pony Club, but is there a master plan?"

Noel hung her head. I wished then I'd kept my mouth shut. I had really put her on the spot and in front of Henry. Noel was so serious in her equestrian ambitions compared to me. I was happy to be a cheerful middle-of-the-road competitor. And it was more than that. Henry! He was the problem. I knew that there was an 'understanding' between them, but it wasn't an official engagement. Henry had said he couldn't marry before he was a captain, and that was at least six years away. Noel was in the awkward position of hanging around until then. What if it all came to nothing?

"Mummy's been at me to do some secretarial work for Daddy. He's writing another book," Noel said lamely. I knew she was just trying to come up with something.

"Gosh! What sort of book? He's not a crime writer, is he?" asked Charles.

"No. He's Professor Kettering, and he's an expert on archaeology," I explained.

"That's wizard!" said Charles. "I remember when I was a kid. I used to cycle around with my friend, Peter, and we'd dig around in the fields looking for old coins. We were sure that we might find hidden treasure." I grinned at him, imagining him as a boy in short pants with a trowel digging away in a farmer's ploughed field.

"How very Enid Blyton," sneered Henry.

At that moment, I felt my love for Charles renewed. I hated the way Henry went all superior. In contrast, Charles was making a Herculean effort to enter into any twist or turn in the conversation. I remembered how Henry had been described as an up-himself windbag in the pony club days. Charles's enthusiasm and boyish cheer were great fun. Henry could be a rather complicated person, and come to think of it, so was Noel, with her quivering nervousness, giving her the semblance of a stricken rabbit. She was in a constant state of flux overcoming her fears which ran parallel to her determination to be a very good rider.

After dinner and a game of scrabble, which Henry won hands-down, we went up to bed. Noel was looking rather gloomy.

"What is it Noel?" I asked when we were alone.

"It's Henry. I'm sure that he's regretting his half-promise for us to get married," she said dolefully. "He's invited me here. So, obviously he's not planning to throw me over just yet. But he hasn't said anything since that last night at camp when we, . . you know."

"Kissed," I supplied the word for her. I was glad that Charles and my relationship wasn't following such a torturous path. "Henry has always been a bit like that. He's got some twists and turns in his character, hasn't he?" I was tempted to add, 'not like Charles', but I knew that boasting about my simple but glorious relationship with Charles was not going to help Noel with her doubts about Henry.

*****

The following morning Noel's world came crashing down around her, and I had no idea how to help. I just stood by, made inane comments, and kept the conversational ball rolling.

Christo Carstairs arrived. She acted as if Radney Manor was her second home. I wasn't sure whether it was her regular visit to ride Echo or the fact that Henry had made it clear that she was welcome at any time.

She was riding her coal-black 15.1 hh mare, Dragonfly. She looked fresh, attractive and full of high spirits, which made it all worse for Noel, who was quite dowdy when she was worrying and nervous about something.

"Good morning, everyone!" said Christo cheerfully. "Susan and Noel, brilliant to see you. And who is this?" she asked.

"Good morning, I'm Charles Ravenscroft."

"How do you do," she called cheerily. "What a sweet mare! Are you all going out for a hack, or is schooling on the agenda?"

She was obviously planning to join us. But, unfortunately, Henry, who could be quite temperamental, was looking relaxed and pleased to see her.

"We thought we might go out hacking. I wanted to show Susan and Charles some of the surrounding countryside. You must come with us, Christo. You're looking well."

I noticed that it was Christo whose appearance he was complimenting, not Dragonfly's. My heart went out to Noel, who was deflating like a balloon the morning after the party.

Christo was very busty and glamorous. Young and strong, walking like a deer stepping confidently through the undergrowth, she shone with health, which was probably the result of playing five sets of tennis before breakfast every morning. She chattered away obliviously, unaware of Noel's discomfort. She was very friendly towards Charles, asking him about Secret and complimenting Noel on the appearance of Truant. She had the air of someone who lived constantly in the sunshine and never considered that the weather might cloud over. What was most evident was Henry. He had been grumpy and sarky at breakfast. Now he cheered up and was quoting poetry and smiling all over the place. My heart sank. I hoped that Noel wouldn't notice, but of course, being hyper-sensitive, she did. She became very quiet, retreating into herself, looking down at the ground. Noel tended to pessimism, but now she seemed to be falling into a pit of despair. Christo was of quite a different character. She always saw the bright side and thrust aside difficulties with careless elan.

Henry told Christo about their plans to go to Birtle Show and invited her to go with them.

"That sounds good fun," she said cheerfully. "I've been schooling Dragonfly a lot. I'm sure she's improved. What do you think?"

"Yes, certainly," said Henry. "Why don't you come over and join in our schooling sessions? We've set up some jumps as well. We're both determined to enter the open jumping."

"Whizzo," said Christo, smiling at him.

We set out on our ride. I had been to Radney Manor when I was a judge at the Radney Riding Club, but the surrounding countryside was unfamiliar. We proceeded down the main road and turned left into a narrow lane. We rode around lanes for at least an hour until finally, we turned off on a bridle path that led across a field full of Jersey cows. They looked very attractive with their black-smudged eyes and golden coats. They moo-ed at us in a curious manner.

"I love those cows. They're so pretty. I imagine they're all called Buttercup and Daisy," I said, flinging out inane comments, trying to defuse the situation with Noel's spirits slowly sinking into the mud. I was furious with Henry, who seemed entirely oblivious to the way in which Noel felt. Charles had ridden up beside Noel, and he was asking her advice about schooling Secret. I was so proud of him. He was sensitive and seemed to understand how she felt. His efforts to distract her demonstrated his chivalrous and thoughtful nature. He was trying to build her up by asking for her ideas and acknowledging her expertise when it came to schooling horses. Noel was definitely the best rider of us all. Henry might be the 'big noise', but it was Noel who had worked unceasingly to improve her standard of horsemanship. She had an inexhaustible thirst for equestrian knowledge.

There was a gate to the next field, but Henry suggested we jump the wall.

"Oh, yes!" enthused Charles. "Let's!"

We circled several times in front of the wall, hoping that the farmer wouldn't mind us riding on his grass and then jumped in single file. Henry, who was the self-styled leader, jumped first, followed by Christo and Dragonfly, who was very forward-going. Then Charles bounced over on Secret, who seemed surprised to be jumping during the middle of a hack but was obviously enjoying herself. Then Noel went over on Truant, and I brought up the rear on Tranquil, who would follow Truant over a cliff if he had to.

Then, we came to a path that ran beside a narrow river, which twisted and swirled beside us. There were more lanes all the way back to Radney Manor. Finch was in the stable yard and helped us to untack and put the horses in loose boxes. Christo came inside for lunch, nonchalantly assuming that she was invited.

"We can school later this afternoon," said Henry. "When the weather cools down a bit. You know, I was thinking Christo, for Birtle, Dragonfly and Echo are the same height. We might as well enter the pairs together."

I gasped out loud. I knew how much this was going to upset Noel.

"We can have a practice this afternoon," said Christo cheerfully. "I've got an ancient aunt coming over this afternoon, and Mummy insists that I show my face to say hello. Would you mind driving me home for an hour or so, Henry?"

"Of course," he said as if this was all a routine matter.

"I must excuse myself. I've got a headache," said Noel, her face crumpling. She dashed from the room.

"Hope she'll be alright to school later today," said Henry.

I could have hit him. He was an insensitive brute.

Charles and I went down to the fir trees at the bottom of the garden and sat in the shade. We took a rug and books and spent a blissful few hours together.

"What are you thinking about?" asked Charles after I had fallen silent.

"Ankle boots made of the finest beige kid leather, soft as skin and decorated with intricate tiny beads," I replied dreamily. "Why? What are you thinking about?"

"I was wondering how people hide in suits of armour. You know there is often a bad person, or even a dead body concealed in a suit of armour. I've had a look at that one in the hall. I can't imagine it would be an easy feat to get into it. I believe you would need a squire. It's certainly not a place where you could hide in a hurry."

"You're quite right," I said. "I've seen that in a movie you know, where someone hides in a suit of armour. You are clever!"

Henry and Christo didn't come back until after four. Noel had trudged down from upstairs looking tragic and unattractive, with red eyes and pale cheeks.

We were having tea on the terrace sitting on uncomfortable white-painted, wrought iron chairs. Henry and Christo were laughing together as they joined us.

"How was the visit with the elderly relative?" I asked.

"She was a jolly old stick," said Henry casually. "Full of stories of when she was a 'gel', and she was a hard woman to hounds."

"Riding side-saddle with bright red lipstick, and all the men adored her," said Christo.

*****

The schooling session went surprisingly well, considering Noel and myself were out of sorts. Charles was confused about the undercurrents, and Christo and Henry were larking around. Truant and Tranquil could match each other almost stride for stride, and we could trot and canter circles sticking together like glue. I wouldn't say I liked admitting it, but Echo and Dragonfly looked well together. They were the same height, one bright bay, the other black. Christo had certainly become a competent rider. Once upon a time, Dragonfly had taken short quick steps with no tempo or cadence. She would never settle. Now she strode out beautifully, with long swinging strides, her head raised but bent at the poll. I remembered how at the Radney Riding Club gymkhana when I had been a judge, Dragonfly had crashed around the showjumping course much too fast, knocking down rails with her forelegs.

"Shall we have some jumping practise?" suggested Charles. He now understood the importance of flat work, but his passion was for leaping obstacles. Secret was in accord with this. She loved jumping as much as he did. They made up for what they lacked in skill and finesse with enthusiasm.

Finch came over to help us set up some jumps. They had been stored in one of the sheds while Henry was away. We dragged them out. There was a wall that had to be manhandled.

"It needs a coat of paint," said Finch critically.

"It's certainly seen better days," agreed Henry.

There was a triple jump which we set at three-feet nine and at least five feet wide; a double made up of wings and poles, which we positioned with three short strides between the elements, or two long strides, or something in between.

"That's a tricky distance," said Charles frowning.

"It's meant to be a challenge," said Henry, adding wooden bricks along the top of the wall so it stood at an impressive four feet.

"Can we have the brush at just two-feet six?" I asked, "something easy and straightforward, to get us warmed up."

Noel had been holding the horses while we worked. She made no comment on the course. Henry didn't seem to notice that she was so withdrawn.

"You go first, Henry," I said. "You can be the path finder."

Henry cantered Echo around the perimeter of the field. The bright bay gelding was certainly going well. There were no more bucking displays like there had been in the early days when he was young and inexperienced. He had grown into a well-built and impressive horse.

"He's a bit small for an Olympic horse," said Christo. "The minimum is 15 hh, but I wondered whether Henry's uncle might have come up with something else for him to ride."

"He's got four years to bring something on and prepare for Mexico," I said. "He's going to have to get some serious experience of Badminton and Burghley if he's going to be a possibility?"

Charles' eyes widened at this discussion. He had never in his wildest dreams thought of riding in the Olympics. That was way out of his league.

Henry turned Echo, and they leapt the brush as if it weren't there, then on to the double, and Echo was bouncing on the spot, bursting with impulsion, taking three small strides and clearing both elements easily. Next, they flew the wall, steadied for the narrow stile, and cleared that as well.

"Oh! Well done!" shouted Christo, clapping.

"He's jumping beautifully," said Henry smiling happily and patting Echo's neck.

Charles was next, and I knew he was nervous to be performing in front of these experienced riders. Secret had no such qualms. She was bursting with self-confidence and bounced around with enthusiasm. Her ears pricked forward, her nostrils flared, and her neck stretched out as she soared over every jump. I tingled with pride. Charles did not have to make excuses. I waited, thinking that if Henry made a disparaging comment, I would literally ride over and box his ears.

"Well done!" he said with a modicum of sincerity.

"That was very good," said Noel earnestly.

It was my turn now, and I pushed Tranquil into his quiet, rocking canter, and we tootled around with no problems, clearing everything by an inch but no more. Tranquil didn't believe in over-exertion.

"You're so relaxed. Tranquil just jumps for you with no dramas," said Noel. "I try so hard, and then I make mistakes. She set off, and her words seemed to have jinxed her. As carefully as Noel placed Truant in just the right place for take-off he couldn't get it right. I think it was a case of overthinking it.

I jumped off, and Charles helped, putting up all the knocked-down poles. To make it worse, Christo jumped a copybook round on Dragonfly.

"Jolly good!" shouted Henry. Charles and I added our lukewarm comments, and Noel was on the edge of tears.

By the time we got back to the house, Noel was wilting. She cried off dinner with a headache and rushed upstairs. Henry paid no heed, and we all sat down to another very mediocre meal with Mrs Thornton presiding over the table, chatting to Christo as if she were one of the family.

Charles and I escaped outside after dinner, leaving Henry and Christo chatting over coffee.

"What on earth are we going to do tomorrow?" I asked, feeling helpless when it came to Noel's anguish. "Even if Christo doesn't turn up tomorrow, there can be no going back. Henry seems determined to hurt Noel's feelings. I could kill him!"

"I must admit it's all a bit beyond me," said Charles. "Perhaps Noel should buck up and come to terms with the fact that Henry is not that keen and move on with her own life."

"Oh, Charles! You're such a sensitive and caring person. You would never do this to me, would you?" I cried.

"I have eyes only for you," he declared. Secretly I wondered where he'd got that phrase, perhaps from a woman's magazine that his mother read.

"Well, if you did behave like Henry, then I'd be putting you straight immediately," I declared.

"You're not like Noel. She seems to bottle it all up and simmer in her own unhappiness," he said. "But it is rather good material for a novel. You know, the delicate interplay of men's and women's relationships," he said apologetically.

"That's the problem," I said. "Christo is so robust and hearty. She doesn't suffer from the finer shades of self-doubt like Noel."

"Perhaps she is the sort of woman that Henry needs to put up with his insensitivity and egotism," said Charles.

We concluded this very grownup discussion with some serious bouts of physical affection. I must say that it was getting rather hot and steamy between us. I wasn't sure where this was all going to go. I knew that it was considered the girl's responsibility to keep things like this in check, but I found myself getting very excited. I couldn't go home and talk to Mummy and Valerie about it. We didn't have that type of relationship, and I didn't think it seemly to try and get advice from my father. Usually, one would have discussed it with a girlfriend, but Noel was in no state to talk about anything like that. Not while Henry was demolishing her delicate feelings in the way that he was.

By the time we got back to the house, Christo had gone home.

"Is she coming again tomorrow?" I asked.

"No, she's playing tennis with the Westcott-Smiths," said Henry. "I was invited as well, but I'll have to stay here to entertain my house guests."

I was on the point of snapping, telling him exactly what I thought of him.

"So, what is the plan for tomorrow?" asked Charles seeing my temper rising.

"I thought we could get up early and do some serious schooling. Echo is going so well at the moment I want to get him ready for some showjumping this summer," said Henry.

"That sounds good," said Charles, for whom the lure of showjumping was strong.

They fell into a discussion about the national showjumper who was on the scene at that time. In a few months, Peter Robeson was the great white hope for the Olympics, and Henry had seen him competing at White City.

I excused myself and went upstairs to see if I could talk to Noel. She needed some moral support. She was lying on her bed looking woeful.

"Oh, Noel!" I cried. "Henry is a pig. I'm so sorry. I think that perhaps you should forget him. You need to get out there and make some new friends. Find yourself a boyfriend who cares about you and appreciates you."

She sniffed dolefully.

The following day, Henry made an announcement as we silently sat down at the breakfast table.

"I'm off to Pevensy Park this morning. Mark Lansdowne wants to show me a horse that he thinks might suit me."

We all looked up in surprise.

"I didn't know you were getting another horse," said Noel. "What about Echo?"

"It's possible to have two horses," said Henry loftily. "Uncle George has promised me a second horse. He's arranged for them to be stabled at livery near the barracks so I can ride while I'm away."

"Gosh! That is exciting," I exclaimed. "What's this horse like?"

"Wait and see!" said Henry smugly.

We set off together in Henry's car. Charles and I snuggled together in the back seat while Noel sat stiff-necked in the front, staring fixedly out the window. Henry was wearing his best riding outfit, pretending not to be excited.

We got to Rychester, then turned off, and followed a narrow road to Langton Shrove. It was a picturesque small hamlet with a village green and duck pond.

"This is chocolate box country," said Charles. I could imagine him memorising details to be used in his writing.

The gateway to Pevensy Park would have been hard to miss. Tall gateposts were topped with gryphons. A small house guarded the entrance. We drove through a park, a luxurious expanse of velvet green grass dotted with spreading oaks with brilliant emerald green foliage.

"Look! Cross-country jumps! Oh, how glorious!" I cried.

I caught a glimpse of the house, which was a delicious golden sandstone colour. There were a host of chimneys and windows glittering in the morning sunlight.We drove on.

"Have you been here before?" I asked Henry. "No, but I got instructions. We're meeting Mark at the stables."

"Gosh! The stables are almost as grand as the house!" I cried.

Mark Lansdowne must have been waiting for us. He strode to the parked car and opened the door for Noel to climb out. He looked the same as he had when he had been a judge at Blainstock, tall, dark-haired, with a hooked nose that seemed to emphasise his arrogance. Admittedly, he was handsome, but I thought there was something sneeringly unpleasant about his countenance. Today, he was undoubtedly making an effort to charm us.

"Good to see you, Henry," he said in a manly, comradely manner. "I think I've got a horse that might suit you."

"Mark, I believe you've met Charles and Susan, and this is

Noel Kettering," said Henry.

We all muttered, 'how do you do' and Charles found his hand clasped by Mark.

He led us to the stable, and there was a tall, brown gelding.

"British Brown," said Mark, pulling off the stable rug with a flourish.

We all looked over the half-door. He was an attractive horse with intelligent eyes, straight, clean legs and a good length of neck.

"He's experienced. I've competed at Burghley twice, and he went well. But unfortunately, I had to retire after being thrown from another horse in the cross-country."

He slipped a headcollar over his head and led him outside. Then, calling Tom, the groom, he asked him to trot him up so we could see his action. I screwed up my eyes, and it seemed to me that his stride was straight.

"Saddle him," Mark said to Tom peremptorily.

I was glad I wasn't a member of the stable staff at Pevensy Park Stables.

Henry mounted and rode around the arena. He certainly looked good on this horse which was considerably taller than Echo. Henry's long legs sat on his sides in a more correct position for giving subtle dressage aids.

 Noel was watching carefully, and I could see her brain ticking over.

"What do you think?" I asked quietly.

"He's well-schooled, obviously. I imagine he jumps well, but there is something a little uninspiring about him. If Henry really wants to get to the Olympics, then he needs to choose something that's got the 'wow' factor."

Henry halted and shortened his stirrups. Then, he turned the big horse towards some jumps that were set up along the edge of the arena.

"He certainly can jump," said Charles.

We had to agree with him. He was a tall horse with long legs and elegant action. Mark stood a little away from us, a hopeful smile playing around his lips.

"If he was an Olympic possible, then there is no way that Mark Lansdowne would be selling him," I whispered in Noel's ear.

"Yes, that was what I was thinking," she replied. "You know I think he is standing over a bit in front, just a trifle, not quite right."

I frowned examining the big brown thoroughbred. I couldn't see anything myself, but I took Noel's word for it. She knew what she was talking about.

At that moment, a huge black horse hurtled across the yard in front of us and burst into the arena. He was ridden by a young girl kitted out in very well-cut jodhpurs and a scruffy jumper. Her hair was streaming behind her, a mane of golden strawberry blonde. Her icy blue eyes, fringed with long black lashes, were flashing.

"I'm planning to jump this morning," she spat at Mark as if he had no right to be there.

The horse that she was riding was coal black without a single white hair. Huge red-lined nostrils snorting, he was bursting out of himself. The girl held the reins like a gossamer thread and seemed to control the huge horse with a powerful personality that defied her slight body.

"What a horse!" gasped Henry in awed tones who had brought British Brown to a halt.

"You sound like you've fallen in love," quipped Noel.

I looked over startled. Then, I saw that she meant he had fallen in love with a horse, not the rider. Henry was standing staring, shell-shocked.

"He looks like a handful," said Charles doubtfully.

"He's a magnificent beast," I said.

"Porsche, I'm sure I mentioned I was showing my horse to these people," said Mark peevishly.

I realised that Porsche must be the infamous younger sister. The shadow opposite of Mercedes who was attractive, impeccably behaved and socially well-adjusted. Porsche was the wild child, a fearless rider who had been responsible for at least one horse's death with her daredevil antics.

"I've finished jumping him," said Henry, "if you would like to take your turn over the jumps."

Porsche flashed him a look that could have soured milk. She bucketed around on the big black horse which was snorting like a warhorse about to enter an arena in a fight to the death.

None of us spoke. We watched the spectacle spellbound.

I saw Noel purse her lips when Porsche sent the horse over the jumps. Her warmup had been all of two minutes, not the requisite minimum of twenty. The black horse, which Mark informed us was called Diablo, leapt every jump with a foot to spare.

"He's magnificent," breathed Henry.

Mark looked annoyed. Diablo made British Brown look ordinary, common place and uninspiring. Henry dismounted.

"What did you think of my horse?" he asked Henry, standing in front of him to block the view of Porsche jumping Diablo.

"He's well-schooled and feels very reliable," said Henry.

"Reliable," echoed Mark ironically. There was defeat in his eyes. He could see that Henry wouldn't buy his horse.

"I'll take him back to the stable," he said quietly.

Porsche went over the course of jumps three times. On the final round Diablo seemed to be jumping more carefully, less extravagantly, heeding Porsche's commands. She rode back towards us triumphantly.

"Would you sell him?" asked Henry.

Noel, Charles and I gasped. Magnificent as was this horse, he was an unlikely Olympic three-day event prospect.

"Sure," said Porsche carelessly. "£5,000 and he's your's."

"I'll write you a cheque," said Henry.

"I'd rather have cash, if you don't mind. Come here tomorrow evening and you can take him away," said Porsche. "But please don't say anything to my family, certainly not Mark."

"Is he your horse?" Noel asked, probably wondering if Porsche had the right to sell him.

"Yes, he's mine," spat Porsche. "I'll give you a receipt. No one will dispute the ownership."

"Aren't you going to ride him?" asked Charles.

"No," said Henry. "I know that he is the horse for me. Come on! Let's go!"

He turned on his heel and we followed him to the car. No one spoke as we drove through the park and into Shrove Langton. Then we all spoke at once.

"What is your uncle going to say?" asked Noel.

"He's certainly fantastic," said Charles.

"What do you think his dressage will be like?" I asked.

"Don't say anything to Uncle George, he's coming to lunch today. I'll tell him that I didn't think British Brown was exactly right. I won't lie. I just won't tell him everything," said Henry. I could see Charles looking uncomfortable. Normally he would have been interested to meet the famous Major Holbrooke but the subterfuge was embarrassing, as if we were all caught in a web of deceit.

*****

The visitors had arrived when we got back. We went upstairs to get changed for lunch.

"What on earth is going on with Henry? To want to buy that horse! It's madness," I said to Noel when we were alone in the bedroom.

"I'm wondering if I even know him anymore," said Noel sadly.

"Perhaps he's just going through a restless stage. He wants to prove himself. Struggling into the skin of the man he thinks he should be?" I suggested.

"I'm wondering if I should say something to the Major. You know, buying that horse could be a terrible mistake," said Noel.

"I think we should respect Henry's wish not to say anything. If he is making a mistake, it might be good for his character," I replied.

"You're right," she said, sighing as if she had the weight of the world on her shoulders.

We went to the drawing room where everyone was assembled. The smell of roast beef wafted down the corridor. It smelt delicious and I wondered if by a miracle Mrs Thornton had managed to prepare a delicious meal.

"I had Mrs Bolton come up from the village to do the lunch," I heard her say. I blushed, wondering if she had read my thoughts.

Henry introduced Charles to the Major and his wife. Charles shook hands in a manly fashion.

Major Holbrooke was a good-looking man for his age, well-turned out with a military bearing. Mrs Holbrooke was thin and elegant with a certain look of wearisome long-suffering. I suspected that this might be the case for many wives of men who were energetic and pursued a passion for horses throughout their lives.

We sat down to an entrée of salad and smoked trout garnished with lemon slices.

"Tell us, how did you get on with Mark Lansdowne's horse today?" asked the Major.

"There was nothing wrong with him. Perfectly good horse, well-trained, jumps well, but I just didn't feel like we clicked," replied Henry.

"So, you didn't make an offer?" said the Major.

"No," said Henry shortly.

"How are you Noel?" asked Mrs Holbrooke. "I expect you and Henry are making the most of his leave."

She said it as if she thought that Noel and Henry were in a committed relationship. I cringed at the thought that she might ask when they were announcing their engagement.

The main course consisted of a huge lump of beef with a crispy delicious skin. The meat inside was a perfect pink. Golden Yorkshire puddings and roast potatoes were complemented by cabbage. A boat of thick savoury gravy was passed around. Then, a pot of horseradish sauce.

We had second helpings and then managed to fit in apple crumble served with thick golden custard.

"I'd be interested to see how you're all getting along with your horses. How about a bit of a show this afternoon?" suggested the Major.

*****

"I feel like we're on parade," grumbled Henry as we rode out of the stable yard.

"I would have given my tack a special clean if I'd known," moaned Noel.

Charles looked a little puzzled. He might have felt as if he were missing something. He hadn't had Major Holbrooke as his Chief Instructor all his life.

We rode around the field. I could see Noel pushing on Truant, sitting up straight, trying to remember not to look down. Charles had his stirrups shortened to jumping length and I wondered if the Major would be interrogating him.

"What's wrong with your leg?" he boomed at Charles.

"I had poliomyelitis," replied Charles in a loud voice.

"I see," replied the Major. "Trot on."

Tranquil trotted quietly, slopping along and I knew exactly what would happen.

"Susan, push that horse on! Legs! Have I taught you nothing in all these years?" shouted the Major.

We trotted and cantered and the major muttered to himself.

"Can I show you something that I've been working on?" said Noel timidly.

"By all means, my dear," he said.

Noel cantered along the long side of the field. Then she changed leg, on a straight line, every four strides. We looked on in amazement.

"Well done, Noel!" I shouted. "That is fantastic. Like something that dressage horse Skydiver would do."

Henry looked bemused.

"You don't appreciate Noel," I said to him.

"You're right," he admitted. "She is the best of us all."

I was mollified. Perhaps Henry was basically decent. He just had problems being his best self.

"Not bad. Not bad at all," said Major Holbrooke. "Truant is coming on nicely. What you really need is some expert tuition."

We waited for thirty seconds as he stood there with a frown on his face.

"Alright, people," he announced. "I can see that Noel has at least been listening all these years. Henry you and Echo are a good team, but he really is too small for you. We must get on to find you something taller. Charles, I like that little mare, very pretty, with a good character I think."

"Well, that was not as gruesome as it could have been," said Henry. He had a faraway look in his eyes, and I thought he was probably dreaming of the demon black horse he was about to buy.

Afternoon tea was not bad. There were cucumber sandwiches, rock buns and shortbread. We all tucked in.

"A friend of mine was telling me that there is a working pupil position at Porlock Vale. I would like to put your name forward, Noel. I think it would give you the opportunity to progress. There is a dressage instructor there, Romanski. He's probably the best in England, perhaps equal to Henry Wynmalen. You could take Truant and you'd get your instructor's certificate, so you'd come out with a qualification."

Noel looked at him in amazement.

"But I couldn't," she stammered.

"I don't see why not," said the Major. "Do you the world of good to get away from Oxfordshire."

I stared at the Major. His idea was brilliant. It would move Noel on from this rut, where she was waiting for Henry to progress in his army career. It would help her to continue to improve her riding, it would give a structure to her equestrian future.

"You *must* do it Noel. It is a fantastic idea!"

I stole a look at Henry to see how he was reacting. He appeared nonplussed.

"I will contact them. I will put my name forward," said Noel hesitantly.

****

I would have liked to stay an extra day to witness the arrival of the demon black horse and see Henry riding him but Charles and Noel were keen to leave. I went along with them. We left Radney Manor the following morning. Noel had rung Porlock Vale and they had invited her there for an interview. They said that Major Holbrooke had recommended her. Henry was barely paying attention when we said farewell. He was off to Radney to withdraw £5,000 from the bank.

I tried to imagine what the Major would say about Diablo. It would have been interesting to know how he rated the horse. We found out later that Porsche was planning to run away from home, and she needed the cash. She was headed to the beaches in Goa in India where there were beatniks seeking spiritual enlightenment in a haze of the best Kashmiri hashish. Such an existence was so far from the shady lanes of Oxfordshire that I found it hard to contemplate. I did doubt that Porsche was going to find much enlightenment, but I had to admire her courage and daring.

THE END

www.ingramcontent.com/pod-product-compliance
Lightning Source LLC
Chambersburg PA
CBHW070936250626
47159CB00009B/3275